HALLOWEEN HORROR SCHOOL

TOBY GLOVER

Halloween Horror School

Toby Glover

Illustrations by Amy Koch Johnson

Future Classics

2

FUTURE CLASSICS
Halloween Horror School
Toby Glover

Published in the United Kingdom by Future
Classics.

1. Evil Teacher
2. Playground Hippos
3. My Home
4. Haunted TV
5. Teacher Tricks
6. The Clown
7. Big Trouble
8. The Football Match
9. The Maze
10. The Holidays
11. The Masterplan
12. The School Trip
13. Where's Junior
14. Rescue Dog
15. The Police
16. The Ghost Dungeon
17. Halloween

18. Mr Brown's Secret
19. Trapped
20. The Chase
21. War of the Ghosts
22. The Ghost Princess
23. Rewards

30 days until Halloween

<u>Evil Teacher</u>

Someone had let off a bottom bomb in class. It was a sickeningly suffocating fog of death that surrounded me. I'd only been in the terrible horror school for ten minutes and already I was being forced to squash my nostrils together and pull my itchy grey jumper over my face to protect my precious lungs from that awful smell. I'm not sure who did it, but the two boys in front of me were elbowing each other and looking suspicious. Some kids are soooo disgusting!

Some of the other kids screwed their faces up and some had turned red from where they weren't breathing, but none of them were smart enough to hide in their sweater like me. It's a necessary act when going to school with stinky kids.

'Good morning Lily,' said Miss Miggs, a terrifying teacher that hovered at the front of the class with long fangs like a dragon; she had hard rotten warts all over her face.

'Hi,' I replied unable to give a full response in case I should inhale some more of that poison gas that was still floating around the room.

Miss Miggs stood bolt upright and her black scruffy hair flung forward across her face. When she walked to my desk and leaned forward menacingly she revealed a thick snake necklace that dangled from her long giraffe neck. Well I thought it was a necklace until it started slithering. 'Young lady at this school we answer the register politely,' she snarled. 'You must say *good morning Miss Miggs* and then tell me what you want to eat.' Her beady eyes peered over her glasses and she was looking through me like I wasn't even there.

'Good morning Miss Miggs,' I replied ever so nicely, and then I added: 'I'm afraid i'm really not hungry as SOMEONE has made me feel sick.' I continued pointing towards the boys in front of me. I was sort of expecting the other children to laugh, but they didn't. Instead it was icy cold quiet. Miss Miggs looked terribly cross.

'What will you be having for lunch today, Lily?' she said slowly as if she was daring me to misbehave.

'I have a packed lunch,' I replied seeing that it would be unwise to wind her up any further. I did, however, need to clear something up and it couldn't wait. 'Please can you call me

Cookies, not Lily? That's what everyone at my old school called me. Only my brother calls me Lily.

'Why the devil would I call you Cookies when it is written here that your name is Lily?' Miss Miggs enquired with her eyes wide open as a vein on her forehead began to pulsate.

'Well I really like cookies and I always have them. I like to eat them so people started calling me the Cookie Monster. Cookies is just quicker,' I said with a smile.

'SEE ME AT LUNCHTIME YOU CHEEKY GIRL!!!!!' screamed Miss Miggs so loudly that the windows cracked and splintered loudly. I promise you they really did break and I always tell the truth.

I sort of wanted to cry or shout back, but I just took a deep breath instead. My brother says that's the best thing to do when you have bad feelings.

Some of the children were glaring back at me in shock, others were shaking their heads and the rest just kept their heads straight down. I don't blame them, Miss Miggs was scary.

I decided it might be best not to talk for the next couple of hours. Nobody else was so I didn't want to break the silence. The problem was the work was really hard; we had this maths lesson and the questions were crazy.

2485683+58253.22-59276.254=

Well I just didn't have a Scooby doo so I put my hand up for help. Instead of coming over and helping me I was smacked on the back of the wrist with an old wooden stick; it really hurt.

'This maths must be too easy for you if you have to put your hand up. Here are some harder questions. Now get on with it!' Miss Miggs said slapping more maths problems on my desk.

'But Miss, I don't get it,' I said and the whole class turned around and hissed at me like rattlesnakes. 'I can't answer them. I'm kind of an idiot you see. I'm probably too stupid for this school; you should really expel me I think. Maybe I should be sent back to my old school? It would be very hard to teach someone as dumb as me Miss Miggs.'

'Get on with your work or you'll get another whack!' she wailed.

'I thought it was against the law to hit kids these days?'

'You're right. I guess you are an idiot if you think that now get on!' said Miss Miggs. (I checked later and it is illegal to hit kids, but she didn't seem to care).

After maths we had English, but all we did was read through this massive old book together which I didn't understand. It was called '101 Fun Facts About 19th Century Dungeons' and a lot of it was in Latin. Oh my days, what a rubbish morning! Not like my old school. At my old school we had a nice teacher; she was funny and kind and helped you when you got stuck.

When lunch finally arrived Miss Miggs kept me in. As the other kids left I felt my heart start beating fast and beads of sweat were dripping down the sides of my head. My hands were trembling and her shadow swallowed me up as she blocked the window.

'We don't talk in this class. We don't answer back in this class. We don't raise our hands in this class. Do I make myself understood?'
'Yes Miss Miggs. It's just I like to have a good old chat. I know it must be terribly difficult for you to have a lot of noise in the class, but I find talking helps me to learn.'

'How the devil could it help? That's the most ridiculous thing I've ever heard. How will you learn to shut up if you're talking? Are you that stupid?'

'No Miss, well sometimes I think I might be. Maybe I am. I don't know. It must be difficult to teach stupid kids. Maybe you should expel me. It would make your life easier wouldn't it?'

'No-one gets expelled from here. We have much better punishments than that,' Miss Miggs grinned.

'I can see that already, but do you really want to have to deal with a stupid kid asking questions all the time and getting the work wrong?'

'Not at all, it will be great fun to give you punishments young lady. I'll start gently as this is your first day and I know you've just come from one of those happy schools, but here we work, we learn and we behave. I'm going to let this be a warning, but if you are rude to me ever again I will send you straight to Mr Brown,' she said.

'Who is he,' I asked timidly?

'Let's hope you never find out my dear little Cookie Monster. Let's hope you never find out. Now go to lunch,' snapped Miss Miggs pointing to the door. 'Josephine, get in here.' She called out.

A shy little girl with light brown skin and an intelligent face peered around the corner and said 'Yes Miss Miggs.'

'Show Miss Monster to lunch.'

'Yes Miss Miggs.'

Josephine began walking out and I followed her. I dared not say anything until we were safely outside.

Playground Hippos

The playground was absolutely enormous and there were huge empty spaces with children clustered in big groups. At one end stood the tall creepy looking school building with it's barred windows, dark walls and heavy oak doors. At the other end was a gigantic muddy slippery field. On either side were deep tall hedges with brambles and nettles.

'This is the playground. Over there you can play football, over there you can skip, over there you can sit quietly and over there you can read the weird books,' Josephine said.

'What's weird about them?' I asked.

'They're not the normal books you find in schools. These are made up by crazy people I think. I moved here from Colombia two years ago and I used to love reading, but the books here are full of lies. You will see.'

'Shall we go and play football? I love football.' I asked changing the subject.

'Best not to,' replied Josephine. 'Only bullies are allowed to play football and there are a lot of bullies here. Some of the teachers give people rewards for bullying.'

'How about skipping?'

'No way! That's a bad idea. The bigger kids swing those ropes so fast like whips and they try to hurt you. I had marks on my legs for weeks after the last time I did it.'

'OK, is there anything we can do that's fun?'

'There is, let me show you.'

Josephine led me past the skipping where I could hear the ropes flying through the air with a crack before they hit some poor boy on the legs and made him whimper. Then we went past the football where I heard shouting and pushing, but no skills. I'm amazing at football. I've got great skills. I thought about how sometime soon everyone would know that, but not today. Then we went past the reading zone where I noticed an African boy looking confused as he turned the pages to a book called 'ALIENS MUST BE STUPID' by Badger Foxhead. Josephine called out to him that we were going to feed them and would he like to come. He jumped up with great energy shouting:

'Mmmm Yeeeah I will feed them. Dinner time.' At that he started laughing so happily.

Josephine walked right up to what seemed to be the edge of the playground and one of the tall hedges. She paused for a minute before pushing her way through the only section with lush green leaves instead of brambles.

'Hallo my name's Junior,' said the boy before pushing his way through too. 'You are in for a surprise'.

I nervously walked into the hedge and foraged forward using my hand to move leaves and see where I was going. I placed one leg deep into the plant life and suddenly I was immersed in it. It felt quite nice and I wished I could stay there and hide from Miss Miggs and the rest of this awful school, but Josephine was calling me. When I stepped out the other side I was in total shock!

Josephine and Junior had turned to one side and were throwing bananas into a huge emerald lake. Swimming towards them were giant, beautiful lazy hippopotamae. I had to blink to make sure I wasn't dreaming. These massive beasts swam up to the bank and then just sat there.

'Take the banana and throw it in his mouth,' Junior said. So I did. I didn't have to unpeel it I just had to aim for the massive mouth of the hippo. One time I missed and none of them moved to get it. They just continued waiting with their huge red mouths wide open revealing their gappy teeth wide open. It was so relaxing feeding the hippos that we forgot to get our own lunch. Josephine said she was really sorry, but I wasn't missing much. I was really hungry though and my brother would kill me if he found out I didn't have lunch. Consequently my stomach was rumbling on the way back to Miss Miggs for art class.

I was looking forward to this though as I thought it might be more fun than the other lessons, but it turned out not to be fun art. We were taken outside and forced to paint this same wall over and over again in horrible brown paint that smelled bad. I thought it might have been hippo poo mixed with water, but dared not to suggest it. The other children didn't speak, so neither did I. At the end I was told we did this in art every week. It was only because I hadn't eaten anything that day that I wasn't sick, I swear. So how would I possibly be able to hold down my lunch next week?

That dreadful day did finally come to an end and I went home feeling very sad. I'd moved to live with my brother a few weeks before. Nobody else was left to take care of me. My brother had to leave his job in the army and become a mechanic so that we could have a home and so that he'd be around to look after me. For a few weeks after the accident with my parents i'd been living with boring strangers who ignored me. I was so happy to be back with my brother where I belonged.

Yet this awful school was going to ruin everything. It was weird and miserable and that was just the first day. Little did I know that this new school would get worse, much worse!

__My Home__

I should probably tell you that it's not just my school that's weird. My home is a little odd too, but in an utterly fantastic wonderful and cool way. First of all I have my brother there, his name is Sam by the way and he's the best brother ever and he's always been like that. Then there's Scraps, he's my dog. He just sort of sits there a lot of the time, but he never argues with me and always listens to all my problems. He really helps me too. When he does get up he runs around chasing his tail and if he sees water he jumps right in. Scraps loves to swim and when he gets out he shakes his fur dry usually soaking anyone standing nearby.

I don't really know how to describe my house. It's definitely not like other houses - it's more of a magic cottage.

From outside it looks so tiny, but when you get inside it's really big. Then there is the magic lever. That is in the comfy room on the ground floor and when you pull it the house grows tall. It goes incredibly from just one floor to six floors. The first floor up is the kitchen, then up further is the bathroom, go even higher and you'll find my bedroom which is decorated with stars and planets because I love outer space. My bed is so comfortable. Above me is Sam's room and then there is the roof where it's cool to hang out as we have hammocks and a telescope up there. We don't have stairs so it took most of the summer to teach Scraps how to use the elevator. The best bit about my home is the garden as we have such beautiful flowers all year round. Besides flowers we also have some Venus fly traps, a ten foot tall cactus and loads of overgrown hedges and long grass. Hedgehogs love to come to our garden as do birds, insects and sometimes meerkats. I love to go out in the garden with Scraps. You can trust me on all of this because I always tell the truth. If you're reading this then you can come around and play anytime and you'll soon see it's the truth.

Anyway, after that awful day I decided to spend some time bouncing up and down on the trampoline before laying down to look up at the clouds. They were all fluffy and I began to see kind faces in them that looked just like my mummy and daddy.

Scraps was sitting down below the trampoline and Sam was cooking sausages and singing rock songs in the kitchen.

'How was your first day?' Sam called from the window.

'Rubbish! I hate that school.'

'What's wrong with it?'

'The teacher is horrible. Not like Miss Bourne from my old school and it's so strict. Most of the other kids are scary,' I said in a sulk. Sam came outside to talk to me more.

'Is there nobody you like? he asked.

'Well I met a couple of nice kids and there were some cool hippos.'

'Really? You know you're not supposed to make up stories Lily.'

'I'm not there were lots of hippos.'

'OK, hippos of course there were hippos. Anyway, just give it time. It's always scary starting somewhere new.

When I started the army I was terrified, but you get used to it.

'I suppose so,' I mumbled.

'I know what will cheer you up. I've cooked your favourite - it's sausages for dinner. They are cooling down on a plate.' Sam was right, that did cheer me up. So we went inside and that delicious smell got stronger and more wonderful as we got neared the kitchen. I was so hungry that my mouth was dripping with hunger and I could almost taste the sausages, but when we went in the kitchen we were so disappointed to see the sausages on the floor and Scraps was gobbling them up. He had run in as soon as Sam opened the door. Naughty Scraps!

'Don't worry I'll make you some bacon and eggs. You can even have cookies for dessert. Go and watch some TV while you wait.'

'Mmmmmm coookkkiiieeess.' I said.

Haunted TV

It didn't take Scraps long to finish off the sausages and he followed me to the TV where he interrupted my cartoons by picking up the remote control in his mouth. He accidentally switched the TV to some boring grown up thing. I was too tired to reach for Scraps to turn it over so now I was watching this strange show about the haunted places of the country. Grown ups are so stupid. Don't they know there's no such thing as ghosts? I really don't think grown ups can be very clever at all. You can see that just by watching grown up TV for two seconds.

Anyway I really was getting bored with it all. This ridiculous man called Simon Spooky was waving his arms around saying he could feel the ghosts and people were showing pictures of ghosts. They weren't real pictures, just pictures with lights in.   You can do that with a mirror. Grown ups are so silly. Simon Spooky was saying an office was haunted. Why would a ghost haunt a boring old office? I decided I couldn't take anymore of this nonsense and was going to turn it off when I recognised the next place they were talking about. Simon Spooky warned it was haunted by more ghosts than anywhere, that it wasn't safe and that everyone had to stay away. It showed big green gates which slowly began to open with a creaky rusty sound that I know I had heard earlier in the day. As the doors opened wide enough I had to blink to believe my eyes. It was my new school. Aaaaaaarrrrrrgggggghhhhh!!!!

Surely they'd been some kind of mistake. Surely they couldn't send children to this place. Surely they couldn't send **me** to this place.

Simon Spooky went through the gates with the camera team and began walking around the school. I didn't recognise a lot of the places, but I froze in terror when they entered Miss Miggs' classroom. They said it was by far the most haunted classroom in the world. **My classroom was haunted**. Just perfect!

'There have been stories about this school for many decades,' Simon Spooky explained. 'We're here to find out the truth. Is there really a skeleton in the library? Are there ghosts everywhere? Are there phantoms in the basement? We've come here to ask the man who will know. We have an exclusive interview with the school Principal, Mr Brown.'

Simon Spooky began knocking on the huge dark door of Mr Brown's office. I could see cobwebs on the wall and Simon Spooky didn't seem like he was just acting scared anymore. He looked REALLY scared. I'm sure I heard his teeth chattering.

'Principal Brown, this is Simon Spooky. We are here to talk to you about the stories and reputation of your school!'

There was no reply and the TV fell utterly silence so that I could only hear the thunder of my heart beating.

'Principal Brown, are you there?'

'Again there was no response for a few seconds. Then came this funny sound and I do mean funny. A strange chuckle it was and it slowly grew louder. It was definitely laughter, but it didn't sound like a human laugh. It sounded just like what a baboon would sound like if it could laugh.

'I'm getting out of here,' said Simon Spooky. 'You said this job was all acting, but this place is scary. There is a weird energy here. I quit. Goodbye everybody.'

Then a voice made an announcement over the show.

'We apologise for the early end to this TV show. We did not expect it. Here is a show about garden gnomes.'

I went running to Sam, scared.

'Sam my new school was just on TV and it said there were ghosts and skeletons and phantoms and the Principal was laughing through a door like a madman.

'Lily you have to stop with these crazy stories,' said Sam.

'It's the truth. Why doesn't anyone ever believe me?' I said starting to cry.

'I'm sorry,' said Sam. 'Of course I believe you. I'll even come to school with you tomorrow and make sure everything is OK.'

'You promise?'

'I double promise. Now eat up, your dinner is ready.'

I forgot all about that dreadful show as I began eating my bacon and eggs. It was delicious. Then came the dessert and all my fears went away and I was just happy with my cookies, chocolate chip, my favourite. It turned out to be a brilliant night. Me, Sam and Scraps went up onto the roof to look at stars and I fell asleep cuddled up in a massive blanket.

29 days until Halloween

Teacher Tricks

You won't believe what those awful people at school did when I went in with Sam the next morning. They pretended to be nice and normal. They even pretended to care about me.

Miss Miggs was of course the worst. We had been shown into the school by Mr Potts the PE teacher and it was the only time I ever saw him when he wasn't running or jogging. Sam told him that I loved sports and Mr Potts promised to give me trials in the football team and the basketball team saying they had been looking for a new shooter.

'That would be brilliant. She is amazing at scoring goals,' Sam said.

'We could even get her a shirt with Cookies written on the back,' said Mr Potts.

'That's really nice of you,' Sam said. 'Doesn't that sound great?'

'If he's telling the truth,' I muttered.

'What a great sense of humour she has,' Mr Potts said with a loud laugh. 'Now let's go and see Miss Miggs.'

When we entered the classroom Miss Miggs was looking less ugly and scary than the day before. She was smiling and wearing nicer clothes. I think it was a turquoise dress and she had on a pretty necklace.

'Good morning Cookie Monster, how lovely to see you,' she said 'and you must be her brother. Please come in and take a seat.'

'Thank you,' said Sam. Sam looked funny perched on the little kids seats with his long lanky legs stretching out to the sides so I laughed at him and then so did Miss Miggs.

'Now, how can I help you' asked Miss Miggs?'

'Well I'm afraid Lily came home very upset last night. I wanted to make sure she was settling in OK and that you were aware of her difficulties. You see she really loved her old school and she's missed it terribly since our parents went away. She can be a little difficult sometimes, but she's the sweetest girl and she needs a lot of kind attention,' explained Sam as I scowled at him for talking about me like I wasn't there.

'Yes she's absolutely lovely and I do feel sad for the poor girl. I assure you we will do everything possible to make sure she is OK and happy.'

'Thank you I really appreciate that,' said Sam. 'I also just wanted to say that she's a little scared. She said she saw a TV show about the school last night?'

'Yes, that awful show about ghosts. Cookies is telling the truth. We can assure you we knew nothing about this film being made. They broke into the school and made up some crazy stories. Then they got an actor to make terrible scary noises from Principal Brown's office. I'm not surprised she is scared. We will be taking the TV company to court.'

'That must have been very bad for the school?'

'Yes terrible, it makes people think we are a bad school, but we try so hard to be good.'

'Can you prove none of it's true? Why would they make it up?' I asked.

'I don't know why people do bad things I'm afraid Cookie Monster. I just don't understand,' Miss Miggs said.

'Well maybe we will both feel a bit better if we could actually meet Mr Brown,' Sam said.

'Absolutely,' said Miss Miggs, 'follow me.'

We got up and out of that horrible classroom and began walking down the long corridors. I peered into classrooms and saw other teachers writing on blackboards and marking books. They all seemed to be on their best behaviour. I could tell it was all an act though for I saw some really creepy things when we went past the library. Some examples of titles on the bookshelf were 'Children Belong in a Zoo' by Derek Flamingo, 'The Mathematics of Cancelling Christmas' by Ebeneezer Misery and 'Making Chocolate Illegal' by Max Fitness. There were giant cobwebs everywhere and it was so dark.

I thought maybe I was imagining it, but I could have sworn I also saw the empty eye sockets of a skull peering between two books. I tried to tell Sam, but he was listening to Miss Miggs explain about how lovely I was and how she thinks I will fit into the school really well. We went past Josephine who said 'hi' and smiled at me.

'I'm afraid that girl can be a bit of a bully,' said Miss Miggs. 'Don't worry we will keep her away from Cookies.'

We finally reached the waiting area outside Mr Brown's office and Miss Miggs instructed us to take a seat.

'I'm afraid I must go back to class now, you just wait here and Mr Brown

will be with you shortly,' said Miss
Miggs. As she left she gave a big smile
to Sam and said 'lovely to meet you'
and 'see you soon Cookies'.

'She seems OK,' said Sam.
'She wasn't like that yesterday,' I
said.
After five minutes Mr Brown still
hadn't come out of his office so we
started getting impatient. Sam said
we should just go in there, but I was
terrified.
I tried to stop him, when he got up
and knocked on the door, but he
wouldn't listen to me. There was no
answer to the knocks so Sam just
barged in. My heart skipped a beat.
'He's not even in here,' said Sam
before opening the door wider so that
I could see inside. There was nothing
really there just a big empty desk
with nothing but a telephone and a

computer, three chairs and a plant in the corner of the room. 'I'm afraid I don't have time to wait any longer. I have to go to work. Are you going to be OK?' asked Sam.

'I guess I'll be fine,' I said.

'When we're both home we'll take Scraps for a nice long walk and then watch a movie. Does that sound good?'

'Brilliant,' I smiled.

When Sam left I started to go back to class, but after a few steps I realised I wanted to check that it really was OK in Mr Brown's office. I hadn't really given it a proper look and I wanted to know what I was supposed to be so scared of. So I retraced my steps and I stood looking up at that big dark door and reached up for the high handle.

I took a big deep breath before pulling downwards on the handle. The door unlatched with a click and opened slightly. I took another deep breath and pushed the door open. It was the same empty office room I had seen just moments before, but this time I decided to go in.

I put one foot slowly into the room and then another. My heart was beating so fast I thought it might explode. I took another step and turned around slowly so that I could see the entire room. It was fine, it was totally empty, but for the desk and plant.

Then I went to the desk to see if there was anything else on it. There wasn't, but I saw there was another at the back. It was white like the walls, so easy to miss, but I'd caught a glimpse of the handle. I just had to see what was behind this mystery door.

It was a round handle and it was icy cold to touch. I twisted it carefully and slowly and then swung the door open. There was pitch darkness so I took a step in and fumbled for a light switch. My hand went through more cobwebs and there was some kind of slimy sick on the walls. It was so horrible, but I'd come this far and I couldn't give up now.

'I eventually found the light switch and quickly turned it on. A big bulb flickered slowly before coming on with an orange dusty glow. I was in a dark dank cupboard that led to some steps. There was no carpet or wallpaper, just brick and concrete. Hanging up on the wall to my right there was a photograph with a sign that said: 'Mr Brown - Horror Principal of the year.' My eyes widened in shock as I looked at the photograph of him with huge smiling lips painted red and his face painted white in contrast. He was wearing a huge red wig, a bright red nose and his eyes were shadowed in black. Hanging next to the photograph was a red, white and yellow clown suit. It had brown and green stains like gravy and bogeys. Mr Brown was a clown.

'Aaaaaaaaarrrrrrrrrrrrrrrggggggggggh hhhhhhhhhh,' I ran away screaming from the room forgetting to shut the door. 'Come back Sam,' I continued. But Sam was gone. The only place to go was back to class and Miss Miggs.

The Clown

I'd been totally right when I thought this school was crazy, dangerous and scary. Not only was Mr Brown a terrifying clown, not only was there a skeleton in the library, not only was Miss Miggs an evil witch who hated me, but there really were ghosts that haunted the school. Junior and Josephine told me all about it at lunch. We were sitting in the big dinner hall eating cardboard cuisine and mushy sprouts. For pudding we were given raw celery.

'Miss Miggs casts spells on you if you're really bad,' whispered Junior. 'One time I called her Miss Mutant and she waved her stick at me. I felt an electric power fly through the air and hit me. I blinked and my eyes got stuck together with crust. You know that stuff in your eyes when you wake up. I had tons of it. I took me four days to open them again, four whole days.'

'And the ghosts are so annoying,' said Josephine. 'One time I did ten pages of maths and then went to the bathroom and when I got back one of them had rubbed out all my answers and I had to start again.'

'What about the skeleton?' I asked.

'He's friendly,' they both said together, 'don't worry about Skelly.'

'But do worry about Mr Potts and don't ever go to any of his clubs. He just makes you run and run laps of the school until home time. If he spots you doing anything wrong he will give you more laps of running to do,' said Junior.

'Whatever you do though of course don't get in trouble with Mr Brown. Children have come back from his office so scared they stop breathing for a while and they don't talk for months. My friend Laura was so scared she made her family move to Vietnam,' said Josephine.

'I'm not scared of Mr Brown,' said Junior. 'He's just a big stupid clown.'

'He's doing a special assembly this afternoon,' Josephine said.

'What? I'm not going. No way. I'm busy, I just can't make it' gulped Junior picking up his tray and running out of the hall.

'How do you put up with all this?' I asked Josephine.

'I don't know. I hate it. I think this awful school needs to be shut down, but whenever any nice grown ups come in the teachers all pretend to be perfect. My mum came in a couple of months ago and they were all so nice to me. I've stopped saying anything bad about it because it looks like i'm telling lies.

That afternoon I was sitting in the hall for the first time with the whole school. Most children sat cross-legged with their heads down, but all the big bullies of the school were standing at the end of the lines to make sure we behaved. I'd met one of them earlier on. His name was Burgers and to look at him I could see why. He'd pushed me out of his way in the corridor and called me Bogey Face. I was so cross, but he was twice my size.

Mr Potts appeared at the front of the hall. He was jogging on the spot as he spoke.

'Now children show your respect for the greatest Principal in the world - the horror headmaster Mr Brown the Clown,' Mr Potts said.

Everyone began clapping as a red mist came down from the ceiling and circus music began to play. Mr Brown entered the room on a unicycle juggling bowling pins.

'Why did the birdie go to the hospital?
To get a tweetment', he joked. All the children did a fake laugh as he continued with his gags.
'What is the best day to go to the beach?
Sunday, of course!
What do hedgehogs say when they kiss?
Ouch.'

The jokes kept coming and they were getting worse and worse. Mr Brown eventually stopped and got more serious.

'Now I have some children on my list who have been very naughty. Some of you have been naughty in class and some of you have been naughty in the playground. If I call you out you must be punished, you will be custard pied in the face.'

'Junior! Come on down.'

'Oh no not again,' I heard Junior groan as he slowly got to his feet and was marched to the front of the hall by Burgers the bully.

Junior stood there for a minute shaking as Mr Brown laughed like crazy before pulling his arm way back and launching the custard pie at a million miles an hour. I didn't even see it because it was so fast. Next thing I knew Junior was laid on the floor covered in custard. He got up and tried to scoop it out of his eyes as Burgers led him back to his seat.

Several more children were custard pied in the face and then Mr Brown looked like he really got cross.

'Now for the really naughty person. One of you brought in an outside person to the school today. One of you told their family about us. One of you even dared to enter my office. For that person we have a special punishment.'

I began to tremble as I realised he was talking about me. I was frozen with shock and my mouth went dry.

'Mr Potts bring on the pool of disgustingness,' said Mr Brown.

'Yes sir,' said Mr Potts. Moments later he returned dragging an inflatable pool full to the brim with revolting liquid.

'Now come here Cookie Monster.'

Before I had time to think I was grabbed by Burgers and this girl called Ladders. I think it was a bad name for her because she was taller than a ladder. She had silver teeth and greasy hair. I'd frozen with shock and didn't have the strength to fight back.

As I reached the front I saw the pool full of liquid which was purple with green lumps floating in it.

'You do not tell anybody about this school. Do you understand?'

'Yes Mr Brown,' I said as the two bullies threw me face first into the filth. The cold wetness froze me and the smell made me feel sick. I closed my mouth and eyes, but some of the muck got up my nose. Disgusting!

When I finally crawled out I was dripping with gunk. The other kids couldn't look at me. Miss Miggs took me to a shower room, gave me a new uniform and told me to be clean and back in class in fifteen minutes.

'Miss Miggs surely you could just expel me?' I pleaded.

'What and miss out on all the slimy fun. I don't think so,' replied Miss Miggs.

The rest of the day was miserable and I was so glad to finally get home. I was scared to tell Sam what had happened and I was worried he wouldn't believe me so I just tried to forget the day and enjoy the brief time I had at home. We went for a lovely walk and watched a brilliant film. Sam cooked delicious spaghetti for me and apple pie with ice-cream for dessert.

When Sam went to bed I told Scraps everything. He always understands. When I finished my story Scraps said 'woof' angrily.

I went to bed and I started to feel angry too. Why had I been so scared? 'Why am I scared of a clown? Why am I scared of custard pies? I'm Cookie Monster and they don't know who they're messing with,' I thought. 'They might have all the other kids scared, but not me. I'm going to show them.

Nobody shoves me in a pool of slime. I'm going to be so naughty that they'll have no choice to expel me. I am the great and powerful Cookie Monster and it's time I took my revenge.'

With these thoughts in my head I couldn't wait to get back to the horror school.

28 days until Halloween

<u>Big Trouble</u>

I scowled at Miss Miggs as she took the register. I was trying to set her on fire with my mind, but it wouldn't work. I couldn't wait to get into trouble.

'Good morning Josephine. Good morning Megan. Good morning Mohammad,' Miss Miggs was taking the register.

'Good morning Cookie Monster.'

'Good morning Miss Wartface,' I replied.

'Ummmmm,' echoed the class.

'You foolish girl. You don't know what you're doing,' said Miss Miggs.

A boy on the desk next to me leaned in and whispered 'you're dead at lunchtime.'

I got really mad and shoved him. I didn't even push him that hard, but he went tumbling off his chair and began rolling around on the floor like he was really hurt. He reminded me of a German footballer. 'Miss Miggs she attacked me. That Cookie Monster girl pushed me,' said the annoying boy.

'How dare you Cookie Monster. He is one of the best bullies in this school. You are not to touch him.'

'I don't care. Leave me alone you wart faced witch!' I said.

'You rude little girl. Now it's time to be punished,' said Miss Miggs pulling out a crooked stick and waving it around. I suddenly had a strange tingling sensation in my arms and legs. It wasn't bad at first, but it got worse. My skin began irritating me all over. It was like I was covered in man-eating ants and it wouldn't stop. I started to itch and scratch but I only had one pair of hands and I was itching everywhere. I got up really fast and tried to satisfy my sore skin by dancing around the place.

'Is that the best you can do? Making me go itchy,' I shouted in defiance. Actually, I hated the feeling and I wanted it to stop, but I couldn't let her know that. Miss Miggs waved this stick again and I couldn't believe it when I felt drops of water on my head. My beautiful hair was getting wet. I looked up to see a rain cloud was forming. It was getting thicker and darker so I tried to move away from under it. It just followed me though and Miss Miggs started giggling an evil cackle. Some of the bullies were laughing too as heavy rain poured down on me.

'I hate you!' I screamed at Miss Miggs as I ran out of the room trying to escape the cloud.

'Come back here. Leaving the classroom equals big trouble,' shouted Miss Miggs following me out. The rest of the class had their mouths wide open as this drama unfolded and I later found out that many of them had run out after us. Everyone was fascinated to see if I would keep being naughty.

I began to run and I turned back to see Miss Miggs was running too. She was really quick for an old lady. I ran into the library and tried to hide behind some books, but they flew up in the air and down to the ground and I was left staring at Miss Miggs again. She was pointing that stick all over the library so wherever I went she would magic things away and was able to see me.

'Two can play at that game,' I thought 'well sort of.'

I picked up piles of books and began throwing them at her as hard as I could. I was still itchy and wet but I didn't care. Just as long as I got my own back just a little bit on the old witch.

'You are the smelliest teacher in the world,' I shouted. 'You are uglier than a rhinoceros bum,' I continued. I could see by the door that children from many classes were now gathered to see what the fuss was about.

'OK you've asked for it young lady. Now it's time for a real punishment. You're going to Mr Brown. First though you're going to find out exactly what it feels like to look like a rhino bottom. I'm going to turn you into just that. Thank you for the suggestion.' Miss Miggs cackled lifting her stick again.

I could feel my face start to·
stretch. It really hurt. My mouth was
getting thinner and then the real
discomfort came when my skull
seemed to be moving and changing.
The pain became so bad I fainted to
the floor.

When I awoke I was staring up at a
talking skull in a top hat. It was Skelly
the skeleton. There really was a
skeleton librarian.

'Don't worry my dear Cookie
Monster. You are safe. At least you
are for a little while. In the library I
am in charge,' said Skelly. I think
that's what he said. I was feeling a bit
groggy and his jaws clacked together
when he spoke so some words were
hard to understand. 'Everyone is back
in class including Miss Miggs. She
knows to behave herself in my library.

I can't believe she came in here at all. You must have really made her mad.'

'I'm good at doing that,' I said.

'Here I have made you a drink. It is made from fresh juices of fruits from all over the world,' he said handing me a posh teacup full of pinky red liquid.

'It tastes like happiness,' I said.

'I guess it does. I've been wondering what to call it,' said Skelly. 'I will call it happy juice.'

'Thanks for helping me I said,' getting off the floor and to my feet.

'No problem. You can always come here if you are in danger, but try not to get yourself in so much trouble, for in the rest of the school I can't help you.

'Can I stay here for the rest of the day?' I asked.

'You can stay until you feel better, but I'm afraid you have been ordered to Mr Brown's room for punishment and there is nothing I can do to stop the orders of Mr Brown.'

For the next hour I had a really nice time with Skelly. He was so kind even though he looked really scary. His eye sockets were big and he had so many teeth. He was terribly well dressed though in an old fashioned suit with a long black coat and a pocket watch. His top hat was very black and clean and he looked terribly clever. It was hard not to stare at his face though, but after a while I began to get used to it. He showed me around the library which included a giant insect collection, a giant globe, an aquarium of skeleton fish and even a bouncy castle at the back of the room. Skelly said he loved to bounce when nobody was around. Then he showed me the books and said a lot of them were not very good and that I wouldn't find my favourites because Mr Brown checks which books are allowed in the school and he has a strange mind.

Skelly took good care of me while I was there and he was a very good host. We played giant Jenga until I started to feel more like myself. As soon as I was feeling better my determination returned.

I was going tell Mr Brown exactly what I thought of him and his scary clown suit then I was going to tell him that I knew he was breaking rules and laws. I had to make my mark in this school or things would never get better.

The Football Match

I didn't have any of the nervousness i'd felt the last time I approached Mr Brown's office. I was totally focused on sorting out this dreadful man and I knew it was him who needed to be afraid.

I didn't even bother knocking, I just barged straight in.

'Yo Brown the Clown what do you want? I'm a busy person don't you know?'

'Hahahaha what a wonderful sense of humour you have Cookie Monster. You're going to need that here. Why don't you take a seat?' said the Clownish meany in his ridiculous suit. Is face was painted a bit differently today. He had a green face instead of white and his hair was fluffier and a brighter red.

'OK get it over with. What's my punishment? Can you expel me? I hate you and your stupid school. Can't believe they let an evil clown be a Principal. My last Principal was a kind man. You're horrible. If you don't expel me I will tell on you.'

'You seem to have the wrong idea about us at this school. Firstly we've never expelled anyone and we've had much naughtier children than you at this school. Secondly it's not all bad here you know? You have been punished for telling your brother shocking lies and I'm afraid you will be punished again for this morning's terrible outburst, but I see great potential for you young Cookie Monster. You have a great spirit and that sense of humour of yours. Yes, I can see how you could make a fantastic bully if you just picked on other children instead of arguing with

Miss Miggs and my self. Mr Potts has already offered to train you as a bully if you will just make a public apology to me and Miss Miggs in this afternoons assembly and then tell your brother you like it here,' said Mr Brown leaning over his desk and speaking in a soothing hypnotic voice.

'What? No way. I would never bully anyone.'

'I've heard that before, but believe me if you give it time you will see things my way. We have special classes for bullies, fun classes. I teach them myself. You can learn to juggle, tightrope walk and ride skateboards while the other children slave away. Mr Potts will pick you for all the sports teams and we have special lunches - delicious lunches like burgers and pizza. I hear you like cookies.

'Yeah I love them.'

'Well the bullies have cookies for dessert everyday. Why don't you start today and all will be forgotten? Why don't you go up to that friend of yours, Josephine? Why don't you pull her hair and call her names? It won't take long, just a couple of minutes.'

'No way Josephine's been really nice to me. I don't want to do that. No.'

'Very well. Don't say you weren't warned.' Suddenly Mr Brown's tone changed and the friendliness went away only to be replaced by a menacing glare. 'Get out of my office now you naughty girl. Report to Mr Potts for football - hahahaha.'

I didn't see this as much of a punishment as I love football, but when I arrived I saw eleven giant kids in boots and full kit in a huddle on a wet filthy slippery football pitch. They were banging their heads together like apes. Mr Potts jogged over to me and screamed at me to get in goal. I looked around at my team. Junior and Josephine were there and so were all the other tiniest children in the school. We were going to get destroyed.

As soon as I stood in between the goal posts the whistle was blown and these hairy gorillas all started charging forward. Junior tried to tackle one of them but he just got run over and trampled. A couple of other kids were flattened until it was just me standing there facing a herd of elephants. The ball was passed to Burgers and he smashed it right at me. It hit me in the stomach and I leaned over to catch my breath before Ladders kicked it hard into my thigh. Boy did that sting and it left a red mark on me, but fortunately the ball spun off and out of play.

The bullies had a corner and they were all so much taller than us. I was getting ready to catch it when Ladders ran up behind me and pushed me over. As I was lying on the floor there was nothing I could do to stop the bully captain, Brontosaurus Bill, heading it in.

Mr Potts cheered and announced the new score even though he'd definitely seen me getting pushed over and the other kids being fouled.

Josephine went to take our kick off and immediately Ladders came over and elbowed her really hard before running at me again. I'd had enough of this so I ran out of goal and did a sliding tackle on Ladders. I got the ball and she went flying up in the air like a somersaulting giraffe. Mr Potts called for a free kick and before I had even stood up Burgers was blasting the football towards my goal.

Just as I thought it was going to be 2-0 I saw Junior flying through the air. He wasn't allowed to use his hands so he fired his body like a torpedo and the ball bounced off his head and onto the cross bar.

'Yes Junior,' I shouted.

I quickly got to my feet and ran after the ball just as it was arriving at Brontosaurus Bill's feet, I clattered into him and we both tumbled over, but I was first to my feet. I spun around and then started running towards the bullies' goal. I could feel the cold air on my face and was splattered by mud as Ladders tried to do her own slide tackle, but I flicked the ball up and leapt over her. I was nearly there, but Burgers was coming to stop me, I thumped the ball through his legs, but he wasn't after the ball. He wanted to squash me, and squash me he did. I bounced off of him and was slammed on the floor banging my head. I could hear my ears ringing and the world was spinning. Josephine came over and helped me up.

'Are you OK?' she asked.

'Yes I'm OK, what's happened have they scored again? I shouldn't have left the goal.'

'They haven't scored, you scored,' said Josephine as I got to my feet. I looked around and everyone on my team was cheering and the bullies were back in their huddle shouting at Burgers and arguing amongst themselves. 'After it went through his legs it went right in the bottom corner. Even Mr Potts couldn't argue with that.'

I shook my head and ran back to goal. Ladders passed to Brontosaurus Bill and he passed to Burgers. Burgers passed back to Ladders and she kicked it as hard as she could. It was headed for the top corner of the goal, so I dived and spread out my fingers as far as they would go. I was so relieved when I felt the ball strike my hand and bounce down to the ground. I dived on top of it as Burgers ran in kicking me. I quickly got up and saw Junior and Josephine had been left unmarked at the other end so I threw it as hard as I could and it landed right at Josephine's feet. She stopped it and passed to Junior who dribbled round the keeper and smashed it in to make it 2-1.

'Yeeeeeeeeeeeeeesssssssssssssss yes yes yes yes yes,' I shouted. Our whole team was going crazy and the bullies started crying. Burgers was the first to shed a tear. He had always been able to bully his way to winning I guess. Then Ladders and the others, they started crying too. Then even Bill started crying.

'Get up, stop crying. It's only 2-1 you can still win,' shouted Mr Potts, but nobody was listening they were on the floor and they weren't getting up.

'I order you to play now,' screamed Mr Potts. 'Look what you've done,' said Mr Potts before he began sprinting off towards the school for back up. 'Mr Brown, we have a serious problem here. We're going to need a new punishment,' he screamed.

My team all danced and cheered, but only until Mr Brown returned.

The Maze

I was barely given a second to rest from the heroics of the football match before Mr Brown came bounding up towards us screaming and hollering.

'Who is responsible for this?'

Everyone on the field including many of my own team mates pointed at me. Then Ladders shouted out, 'it was Junior and Josephine as well. They were cheating.'

'No we weren't you're just bad losers,' said Junior.

'Right Junior, Josephine and Cookie Monsters follow me,' ordered Mr Brown marching off back towards the playground.

We nervously followed him and with every footstep the sky became darker and more menacing. The clouds became black and the first rumbles of thunder echoed through the sky like the burps of a Tyrannosaurus Rex. I guessed we were headed for the playground, maybe to those skipping whips, but Mr Brown stopped about 100m before the playground hedge where I had been to see the hippos.

'Oh no, oh no, oh no,' said Josephine as Mr Brown spookily turned right like a soldier, slumped to his knees and then fell forwards flat on his face. He put his arms out in front of him and began army crawling under a bush until he completely disappeared.

'Follow me,' he barked.

'I hoped this would never happen to me,' said Junior as he also got down to the floor and crawled under the bush.

'Tell my family I love them,' said Josephine as she crawled under too.

I followed them and began making my way under the bush where I was stung viciously by nettles and when I looked at my arms I had been immediately covered in big ants. I sped my way through and out of the other side so that I could shake away those yucky insects. When I was finally free from them I looked up to see Josephine had a massive slug on her back.

'Don't move,' I said. Honestly this slug was about the size of a small cat and it was clinging to her like a backpack. I grabbed hold of it on either side and felt it squidge and slime in my hands.

'What is it?' asked Josephine 'please get it off.' It was really stuck on good and I had to pull so hard that when it finally came off I fell to the floor and it landed on top of me covering me in slime. I got up as fast as I could and kicked it like an American football as I heard Josephine screaming. It was like slow motion as I saw the giant disgusting slug spiral through the air and head straight for Mr Browns clown face. It was twisting and turning and eventually it landed flat onto his face. I heard these awful murmured groans coming from him and he fell to his knees once more trying to tear it off his face. When he was finally free of it his make up had been smudged and the big red smiley face had been wiped off to reveal a sad and furious face.

'You awful girl. You are now on my enemy list Cookies. No more chances to be a bully. No more friendliness. You are in big trouble. Time for the maze. Let's see if you are so naughty after this.'

Thunder crackled in the sky again and it was much louder this time. I still hadn't heard any lightning, but I could feel the electricity in the air.

Ahead of us was a large tall hedge with an entrance.

'You will go into this maze and once you do we will seal off this entrance with bullies. You must make your way to the centre of the maze. When you do, you will find a tunnel that will lead you underneath the school and back into my office. You will not be alone, you will be joined by the hippopotami,' Mr Brown explained.

'They won't hurt us. We've been feeding them and they like us,' said Josephine.

'Correction they did like you, but they've found out what you've been saying about them. Miss Miggs is telling them right now,' Mr Brown said.

We looked far into the distance and saw Miss Miggs standing by a fence making hippo noises. If you hadn't seen her you would really think it was a hippo making those noises. Behind the fence were the hippo's and they looked really cross. They were staring at us and some were pacing around in a mood. One of them was rubbing his foot against the floor as if he was getting ready to run at us.

'What is she telling them?' Junior asked.

'That you three said the hippo is the stupidest, ugliest, smelliest and laziest animal there is. Even worse than a dung beetle,' Mr Brown answered as Miss Miggs opened the gate and the huge powerful animals began charging towards us.

'Run, get into the maze now,' shouted Josephine as the first bolt of lightning flashed in the sky. I didn't really need this advice as I was already sprinting as fast as I possibly could through the door of the maze and turning this way and that.

'Keep up, we have to stick together,' I shouted turning back to encourage my friends, but it was too late they had already taken different turnings and I was on my own, so I just kept legging it. I had no real aim as I had no idea where the middle of the maze would be. It appeared so enormous. I just wanted to get as far away from the animals as possible.

I began to feel the first drops of rain fall on my face as I ran in utter terror, my heart was beating so fast and I couldn't catch my breath. I'd never been so scared and as the rain went from small drops to huge torrential blobs of soaking water, I began to cry for the first time at this stupid school. Lightning forks were flashing in the sky and the thunder deafened me and made me shudder in fear. I couldn't run any further, I just couldn't, my legs were burning and my lungs were in pain. I could hardly breathe so I found a corner, closed my eyes and hid, hid from everything, from the teachers and the bullies and just waited for the hippos to come and squash me. As the tears dripped down my face and the awful rain soaked me to the skin I felt a hand on my shoulder. I looked up to see a walking, talking scarecrow. A real life human made out of straw would normally seem unusual, but after a couple of days at the horror school nothing seemed shocking anymore.

'Please stop crying. My name is Paige the Crow Scarer, but please let me warn you that everything I say is a lie. I can't help it as Miss Miggs put a curse on me, but I can tell you that the middle of the maze is straight down there, and then you turn left and then you turn right.'

'What. How can I listen to that if you always tell lies? I'm better off here.'

'OK, don't say I didn't try. Josephine and Junior have already safely found the middle of the maze and are headed back to school and I should say the hippos will be right here in about thirty seconds,' said Paige.

'I don't believe you. Hang on if you always tell lies then I just have to do the opposite of what you say.'

'Yes you do,' said Paige as I thought hard and long.

'So I just have to go the other way, and then turn right and then turn left and I'll be there. Thanks.' So I turned around to get there quick, but I was immediately faced with a giant hippo and he was staring at me breathing deeply through his fat nostrils.

'You said he'd be thirty seconds. That must have been almost exactly thirty seconds,' I said.

'Yes,' said Paige.

'You also said you always lie, that must have been a lie too. Maybe you always tell the truth.'

'But then I'd have been lying about always lying. I'm sorry Miss Miggs is very smart and her spells are complicated. Either way I would run if I were you,' Paige said as the hippo began charging for me. 'I think maybe I should too,' continued Paige as he realised the hippo was also headed in his direction.

I sprinted the way the Scarecrow had told me and I could hear him running behind me until he let out a big scream and his

head went flying through the air in front of me and landed on the floor.

'Run, run, run,' said Paige's disconnected head as I screamed for my life.

I turned left and then right and there was the tunnel just ahead of me. I could feel the hot breath of the hippo on the back of my legs before he smashed his big head into the back of me and I went flying through the air. I landed right at the entrance and pulled myself into the tunnel as fast as I could. When I was far enough in I dared to look back. You wouldn't believe the relief I felt when I turned round to see the hole was too small for the hippo to fit through. His big face was stuck staring at me, and his mouth was wide open. So I went back and gave him a little slap round the face for chasing me and called him a naughty boy. His angry face relaxed and he started to cry.

'Well you shouldn't go around chasing children in mazes,' I said. The hippo let out a strange hippo moan, but it sounded like sorry. Anyway, I headed through the tunnel and back to school.

I was greeted by Junior and Josephine. They had got back quicker but Junior had a big hoof print on his back and Josephine said a hippo had sat on her with his big butt. They both looked like they needed a doctor, but instead we were sent to Mr Potts again and forced to run twenty-five laps of the school field in the pouring rain. When we got to the twenty-third lap I was sick everywhere, but they wouldn't let me stop even though it was pink puke like the rhubarb custard I'd been forced to eat at

lunch. I just had to keep running.
When we reached the end Mr Brown,
Miss Miggs and Mr Potts were all
standing waiting for us.

'Now are you three going to behave
yourselves from now on?' Miss Miggs
asked.

'Yes,' said Junior.

'Are you going to respect the
bullies, the teachers and me?' asked
Mr Potts.

'Yes Mr Potts,' Josephine said.

'What about you Cookie Monster?'
asked Mr Brown.

'Why can't you expel me?'

"We don't kick children out of this
school. It's against our policies. Now
are you going to behave?'

I thought for a long time and then
swallowed my pride before saying, 'Yes
Mr Brown'. I couldn't take anymore of
these punishments. So, as much as I

hated Mr Brown and the whole school
I decided to behave.

For the rest of that week and the
one that followed I didn't make a
sound. I walked around quietly, I eat
quietly, I read quietly and I worked
quietly. When bullies made fun of me
I didn't react, I just took it. When I
saw teachers being unfair or nasty I
just ignored it. I became a robot. I
just wanted to get to the end of the
week without any trouble as the
autumn holiday week was coming and
even though I'd only just started this
horror school I was definitely ready
for a much needed break.

14 days until Halloween

The Holidays

I had such a good week away from the dark and damp misery of that old miserable building with its huge towers and icy bricks. The cobwebs, the smell of poo in the toilets, the taste of bogeys in the dinners and the sore bum I got from the uncomfortable chairs.

I was free from it all and it was wonderful. I could stay in my bed for ages in the morning and I could eat nice food. Sam took the week off and although I spent some time helping him fix cars we also went to a dinosaur themed adventure park where we went on the Megadactyll coaster that shot you up and down and round in the air. Then we went on the Horrosaurus ride flying down a Sauropod neck and into a big lake where you get splashed with water. I had a T-Rex burger and triceratops candy and stegosaurus candyfloss. It was so yummy. We stayed until it got dark and then went on bumper cars and saw this amazing fireworks display that lit up the sky.

Another day we went to the zoo and saw all these incredible animals like dolphins that did tricks and giraffes that we got to feed. One of the giraffes ate some food pellets out of my hand and its tongue licked my fingers. It was soooo disgusting!

Every morning and evening we would take Scraps for a long walk in the countryside where he would run up to trees and bark at them. We would kick balls and he would race after them. We found this giant hill that I liked to run up to the top of and then roll down. I got really fast at rolling down hills. I think it's very good exercise and fun too. Sometimes Scraps would race me down to the bottom of the hill, but I usually won. Sam would wait at the bottom laughing at us. I love the autumn time as it's so cosy and nice. I had so much fun on our walks throwing leaves around and rolling in them. I like getting muddy and dirty.

In the evenings we would have a lovely delicious dinner and then watch movies or read stories about far away magical Princesses and Princes. Other stories were about knights and dragons, some of them had ogres and wizards. I loved reading all these stories that had been banned from the Horror school as I had missed them terribly. My old teacher used to tell us amazing stories. Sometimes

Sam would light a fire and we would toast marshmallows.

We also went up to the roof a lot to look at stars. It was getting colder and darker so it was great for stargazing. One night we could see Mars and I wondered what it would be like to live there. If there was water and shelter I'd like to live on Mars I think.

I felt really grateful that Sam was my brother. He never complained or looked sad and he would always do fun things and have exciting ideas. He liked building things and had plans to make me a go-kart and a tree house. He's the best brother in the world. I also have Scraps and he's the best dog in the world, but it's not enough. I miss my parents so much and the pain is dreadful. They went away not long ago. People said it would get better, but it hasn't. Most nights I cry and every night I pray to see them again, but I'm still waiting. I hope they are safe wherever they are. I'll try not to mention it again as it just makes me sad. I'll try to stick to the story of the Horror school.

I think it was on the Thursday of my week off that I got this mysterious message over the internet. It was from Josephine. This is what it said.

To- cookiemonster@spookynet.com
Subject- Top secret
Cookies,
            Big secret. Could save us. Junior found evidence. Meet tomorrow at 2pm. Ghost park. Come alone.
From Josephine.

The last thing I wanted to do was think about school let alone talk about it, but could I really carry on the way things were? I'd only been there a couple of weeks and it had been so hard. When I tried to fight it just got worse. Maybe I was better off just keeping my head down. Yet maybe Junior really had found something and we could go to the police. After a lot of thought I remembered who I was. I wasn't a victim of bullies and I wasn't a victim of anybody. I had to continue to stand up for myself.

So I replied

Hi Josephine,

I'll be there.
Let's sort this out.
Cookies.

13 Days Until Halloween

<u>The Masterplan</u>

I was the first to arrive at the park and it was empty and so quiet. I felt nervous being there and I was angry at Junior and Josephine for making me come to yet another creepy place. It was supposed to be daytime, but it felt pretty dark to me and i'm sure I could hear owls hooting in the distance. I wished i'd stayed at home to help Sam fix cars.

I didn't have to wait long though until Josephine turned up with her big white smile and her long dark hair. I'd only seen her before in school uniform, but today she was wearing jeans and a hooded top and looked much cooler. I wondered what I looked like at school. Terrible I expect.

We said hello to each other before noticing a suspicious figure in the distance coming towards us. He was walking with a purposeful stride, but was cautiously turning his head from side to side like a zebra who thought he might be in lion territory. As he got closer we could see he was wearing sunglasses, a hat, a long black coat and was carrying a briefcase. He looked like a government secret agent, but he was way too short. I thought about suggesting to Josephine that we should move away from this guy, but when we did begin to back away he shouted a really loud whisper at us.

'It's me, it's Junior ssshhhh.'

'There's nobody here Junior, why are you whispering?' Josephine asked.

'You don't know there could be bugs in the tree.'

'What like woodlice?' I said.

'This is no laughing matter. I am here on top secret business,' said Junior taking off his sunglasses and coat to show that he was wearing a tuxedo.

'You're really taking this seriously aren't you'?

'Are you supposed to be James Bond?' Josephine asked.

'Don't talk to me of James Bond. All those movies are based on my life. I am taking them to court. James Bond is really Junior Basco. JB, it is a rip off of me.'

'Really? Those movies are old. You weren't even born when they came out,' I said.

'I mean it's my dad. He's the real James Bond. Then he taught me everything he knows.'

'I see,'

'Anyway I don't have time for this. Here is what I have come to show you.,' Junior said as he began to unlock the briefcase.

'What's in there? Your sandwiches?'

'Well yes, but also the evidence we've wanted for so long. Proof about what the Horror school is really like. Proof about Mr Brown and Miss Miggs.'

'What is it'?

'It's a contract. An agreement of teaching,' Junior said as he pulled out an old brown piece of paper with tattered edges and brown stains that was rolled into a cylinder. 'You see when a teacher starts working at a school they have to sign a piece of paper agreeing to the job. Most of them are very normal boring things about working hard, being nice to children and making interesting lessons. But this is for Miss Miggs' job, and it was written by Mr Brown. It speaks of all the strange things about the school, the horrible attitude of the teachers, the preference of the bullies, the scary things that live in the school, everything. And what's more it has the signature of both Mr Brown and Miss Miggs.'

How did you get it?' Josephine asked.

When you two were still in the maze, they were worried the hippo might have really hurt me. They were worried my mum would come in to complain. My mum is good at telling people off. Even Mr Brown doesn't want to be told off by her. So they sat me in Mr Brown's office while he was waiting for you and one of the teachers cleaned up the bruises and scratches. It really hurt and I said I was going to faint. She said she didn't know what to do so she went to phone a friend who was a nurse. While she was gone I looked through Mr Brown's desk and right at the back I found this, this golden ticket, this wonderful piece of paper. We're going to get the school closed down once and for all.'

'OK let's read it and see if it's as good as you say it is,' I said.

Regarding the employment of Madeleine Miggs at the Halloween Horror School, following a superb interview and previous experience we would like to offer you the job of class teacher and behaviour mistress under the following conditions.

1. *You do not talk about the Halloween Horror School*
2. *You do not talk about the Halloween Horror School EVER!!!!*

3. You are never to punish a child who is bullying or making another child's life difficult.
4. You are never to make lessons interesting or entertaining.
5. You are to provide boring work that is too difficult for the children on a daily basis.
6. You are never to disturb ghosts, phantoms, skeletons or other disbelieved mythical figures that live permanently on school property.
7. You must harshly punish any child who questions the methods and culture of the school.
8. You will not allow fun, jokes or smiles (It will spoil it for when they hear the Principals wonderful jokes).
9. You must send extremely naughty children to Mr Brown.

10. You are to act kind, caring and
    considerate if ever you should
    meet a parent or carer.

  Additional duties- you must write
reports once a term (all bad), you
must keep your classroom tidy and you
will be paid extra to look after the
school hippos.

  Signature of employer- *Duncan
Brown*
  Signature of employee-
Madeleine Miggs

  'This is it, this is perfect,' I said
jumping up and down with happiness.
  'I know yeah, the best. Now we can
go to a wicked school, a brilliant
school. We can learn and make friends
and be happy,' Junior said giving me a
high-five.

'Hold up guys,' interrupted Josephine. 'How can we prove this isn't fake? The police might think we wrote it then signed it. We need to be able to prove that this is Mr Brown's handwriting and Miss Miggs' signature.'

'How are we going to do that?' I asked.

'Miss Miggs will be easy. One of us will just have to ask her to sign our homework because our parents don't believe we've handed it in. I'm not sure about Mr Brown. One of us will have to go back into his office I suppose and get some more of his handwriting. Most of his letters are done on the computer.'

'I'm not going back in his office,' said Junior. 'I've done enough. One of you two should go.'

'One of us will have to go in there. Someone will have o go in and either take something or get him to write something down,' I said.

'How do we decide who does it?'

'Rock, paper, scissors,' I suggested. So I went against Josephine first. 'Rock, paper, scissors,' I said as we waved our fists down three times before revealing what had we'd picked. I went for scissors and Josephine was a .... Oh no a rock, rock beats scissors. 'Best two out of three,' I suggested.

'Sorry, no thanks,' Josephine said.

'So now it was me against Junior and we waved our fists down three times again and I decided to stick with my plan of scissors and Junior was ...... paper.

'Yes, scissors beats paper.'

'Oh no why is everything always me? I don't believe this. I'm going to get caught I know it. OK see you in school I will get more of Mr Brown's writing,

but you two need to get Miss Miggs'
signature,' Junior said.

'Deal,' said me and Josephine as
Junior closed his briefcase and put
his coat and sunglasses back on
before walking off muttering to
himself.

'I'm going to get caught, I don't
believe this. Not Mr Brown again.'

I felt bad for Junior, but I was so
glad it wasn't me that I couldn't help
but laugh.

8 days Until Halloween

The School Trip

Getting Miss Miggs to give her signature was convenient and easy. We had a school trip coming up to the circus and some caves and Sam wanted to pick me up straight from there to take me to the dentist. He wrote a letter that Miss Miggs had to sign saying that she understood this was happening. She didn't look happy about it though and she scowled when scribbling her name. When we checked it the signature was identical with Junior's document and I made sure to make a copy of it in the library before returning it to Sam.

Junior wasn't doing so well and by the time the school trip rolled around he still hadn't worked up the courage to go back into to Mr Brown's office. I was beginning to think I would have to do it myself.

I'd been looking forward to the school trip as the circus and the caves sounded brilliant, a wonderful distraction from the routine hell of the horror school. Yet I should never have got my hopes up. Nothing was normal about the school, not even the outings.

We lined up in single file to board wagons that would take us to the circus. They looked like they normally carried hay, not children. We had to sit on the dusty floor and then were dragged along old bumpy, cobbled roads at such a fast speed that we were thrown up and down all over the

109

place. It was soooo uncomfortable! We finally stopped in a big field and when I got out I saw what was supposed to be the circus. It was a big tall marquee with faded colours and was held to the ground by rusty pegs. I guess it looked much the same as any other circus tent, but the cold wind that sent chills down my spine and the sight of Mr Brown leading us into the tent made me think otherwise.

Inside we were instructed to take our seats in the audience that stretched around a performance area. When everyone was settled and quiet the strange show began with Mr Potts walking to the centre of the stage limping and hobbling with a walking stick. He had a sad lonely look in his eye and he was staring off into the distance as if he had no idea where in the world he was. He suddenly dropped the stick and began falling backwards like a tree falling in the forest. Yet before he went splat on the floor he adjusted his body and went into a backwards roll and then stood up to do a double pike somersault where he landed flat on his feet before going into

the splits, rolling back onto his shoulders and springing back onto his feet and grabbing a microphone.

'Boys and girls, prepare for a treat, the greatest show on earth is here at your feet,
the Horror Schools show begins now with me Mr Potts,
and my amazing dancing acrobatic baboons are here on the dot,' said Mr Potts as a troop of red bottomed baboons came somersaulting on to the stage from every direction. Some of them even abseiled down from the ceiling. They performed an incredible dance routine around Mr Potts who was break dancing as the baboons jumped, leaped and rolled around him with exquisite timing and style. At the end of the song the baboons all stood on top of each other in a giant baboon pyramid.

'You may clap,' said Mr Potts and boy did everyone clap. As much as I hated Mr Potts I had to hand it to him that was quite a show. My warm feelings didn't last long though as soon after I saw a giant baboon poo falling from the pyramid. Mr Potts was not happy when it landed on his head. 'You stupid baboon. You've ruined it. I've been working on this all year and you've ruined it. He picked up his stick and wacked one of the bottom baboons and the pyramid collapsed. The apes made a terrible noise as their red butts went tumbling to the floor. It looked really painful for the ones at the top and they were mad with anger. The baboons started jumping and chasing Mr Potts as he sprinted out of the circus with a big poo on his head.

Next to perform was Miss Miggs as a snake charmer, again I was genuinely impressed. There were hundreds of terrifying snakes slithering around the floor and they all followed her in a hypnotic trance. Towards the end the snakes all turned to face the crowd in a big circle and began headbanging to some rock music and then they were swaying back and forth to a love song. Finally Miss Miggs called out 'disappear,' and a huge bang of fire and smoke made me blink. When I opened my eyes the snakes were gone.

There were several other acts including a trapeze artists, a bearded lady, a sword swallower and a freak show. The freak show was just people and animals with deformities. I thought it was mean to bring them out let alone call them freaks. I'm pretty sure it was illegal anyway.

The last act of the show was of course Mr Brown who appeared on a tightrope suspended high above the floor. He walked across it effortlessly in his clown suit only stopping to launch custard pies down on the audience below. I was lucky not to get hit this time, but the girl next to me got a pie right in the face and she couldn't see for about ten minutes. When Mr Brown got to the other side he climbed onto a unicycle and rode back across before sliding down a pole where he got into a tiny little car and began driving round the place telling these awful jokes. He did it for ages and I got so bored that I guess I must have fallen asleep.

'Wake up!!!!!,' screamed Mr Brown. I woke up sharply and sat bolt upright. Luckily I wasn't the only one who fell asleep. Most of the school had. 'You annoying children just don't understand how funny my jokes are. There is something wrong with you all.

Forget it. No more circus. We're going to the caves.

We were ordered to go outside and line up in silence, but Junior was behind me and he wouldn't stop talking.

'I've got it,' he said 'I've got it.'

'Sssshhhh you're going to get us in trouble,' I replied.

'Who cares? I've got it. While everyone was asleep I sneaked out and back here. I found Mr Browns bag with his bank book. I've got his signature. Not only that I've got details on how and when he brought the clown costumes, the animals, the gunge pool, the maze, the custard pies, the strange books. Everything. I've got everything, and I'm going to the police, tonight.'

The Caves

We were loaded back on to the wagons where we were given warm water and a stale crusty cheese sandwich.

'Oh my days I'm so thirsty' said Junior after he guzzled down his water in one go. 'Can anyone give me some more water?'

Several people came to aid saying it was warm and disgusting and that he was welcome it. Junior drank bottle after bottle as if he hadn't had a drink in years.

'Why are you so thirsty?' asked Josephie. She had kindly given him her water.

'I don't know I just can't get enough,' he said, swigging his last bottle and turning it upside down to get the last drop before a look of panicky realisation suddenly came across his face. 'Miss Miggs. Whenever something strange happens it's always Miss Miggs!'

'No, why would she make you thirsty?' I asked.

'I wouldn't be surprised if it was her. One time she cast a spell that made me really hungry and she made me think mud was delicious. I ate loads of it,' said Josephine.

'Oh no what's going to happen to me? They know don't they?' groaned Junior.

'They don't know anything, it's all in your imagination,' I said.

We continued driving for what felt like forever. My bottom was really starting to hurt, so when we finally arrived I was mightily relieved. When we got out I couldn't see any caves though, in fact I couldn't see much of anything apart from a big open field that ended in a cliff overlookingg the sea. I couldn't believe it when we headed in that direction. Mr Brown was walking really fast and we were expected to keep up. I looked back to see Burgers miles behind everyone else puffing and panting. Mr Brown just kept trudging forwards until he reached the edge of the cliff. He waited until we were all there and then he grabbed the first kid and wrapped a big rope round him, tied it at his waist and then threw him off the cliff.

'What are you doing?' I shouted.

'Ssshhhh' said everybody else.

'Somebody call the poli.....mmmm,' I continued until my mouth suddenly closed shut and I couldn't talk. I looked around and Miss Miggs had her stick pointed at me. Mr Brown was still holding the rope and was now swinging it from side to side then he pulled it up before grabbing another child and tying the rope to them before launching them off the cliff. He got quicker and quicker at this until one child was launched off the cliff every ten seconds. Miss Miggs and Mr Potts began abseiling off the cliff as Mr Brown continued grabbing child after child. I tried to scream when he grabbed me and pulled that big thick rope round me. I wanted to call for help as he threw me off the cliff. I began to fly through the air and I saw the big blue sea rushing up closer and closer towards me. There were eagles soaring upwards, but I was plummeting down. I was suddenly halted in mid air and began swinging from side to side before being thrown forwards in one big swing. As I began going backwards again I worried I was going to go smashing into the cliff wall. I closed my eyes and prepared for the painful impact.

Instead of hitting the wall I landed on the floor with a soft thud. Mr Brown had swung me into a cave where Mr Potts was waiting to untie me from the rope. The other children were lined up and ready to explore the caves. A few minutes later everyone was in the cave and Mr Brown's clown suit emerged from behind us.

'mmhhhmmm did you get in here?' I asked Mr Brown as my mouth finally opened.

'Ssshh Cookies let's begin the tour,' he replied marching into the darkness.

It got really dark incredibly fast. The only light we had was from Mr Potts torch and Mr Brown's bright red neon clown nose.

'These caves have been used by ghosts for thousands of years,' began Mr Brown, 'but the first clown wasn't spotted here until 1879. Witches have also lived in these caves dating back to the time of King Henry the First. If you look carefully you may come across a cauldron. Nice people were not allowed in these caves until 1973 and to this day they must be escorted by a witch, a clown or a phantom so you are all very lucky children. During World War 2 some nice people tried to hide here and they were never seen again! Some said they swam to France and others said they just never found their way back up to the top of the cliff.'

I had to hold my hands out in front of me and try to feel where I was going, but mostly I just kept bumping into Josephine.

'Ouch!' she exclaimed as I accidentally trod on her foot, banged into her head and fell onto her back.

'Sorry' I said several times, but I had a kid falling on me from behind as well. The floor felt squidgy under my feet and when I touched the walls they were cold and wet. I walked through several spider webs and began to worry that insects were everywhere as Mr Brown continued his lecture.

'The caves have been eroded by the sea for hundreds and thousands of years,' said Mr Brown before he was interrupted.

'Mr Brown please stop. Where are the toilets,' Junior cried?

'No stopping, said Mr Brown.

'But Mr Brown. I'm desperate.'

'You can hold on,'

'I can't! I'm going to wet myself. I've had so much water. Please where are the toilets?'

'Very well, Miss Miggs can you show young Junior to the toilets?'

'Certainly,' said Miss Miggs as she grabbed Junior by the scruff of the neck and marched him off into the darkness.

The tour continued and I began to feel very cold. We stopped to sit in the darkness for another massive lecture about cave paintings. I thought I was going to freeze to death. I dreamed of a hot bath and hot chocolate, anything hot would do. Yet we had to march for another few hours until we finally reached a slippery slope that meant we had to army crawl up. Suddenly we were covered in blinding light as Mr Brown opened a drain cover and we began filing out into the open like rats coming out of the sewers.

'Why didn't we go in this way?' I asked.

'Where's the fun in that?' said Mr Brown? 'Right! Back on the wagon.'

'Wait, what about Junior and Miss Miggs?' asked Josephine.

'Miss Miggs messaged me to say Junior was feeling terribly unwell so she has already taken him back to school.'

I was glad I didn't have to cram onto that horrible wagon again. Sam was waiting for me in his amazingly clean smooth car. Unfortunately he was taking me to a new weird dentist that sung old fashioned songs. My life is sooooo unfair!

7 days until Halloween

Where's Junior

After the dentists I spent the whole night anxiously checking the news to see if there was a big story about the Horror school, but there wasn't. I didn't get any messages from Junior or Josephine so I worried that maybe the evidence had gone missing.

At school things were just normal and the boring, impossible lessons continued with everyone in total silence. The only odd thing was that Junior wasn't there. Was he really sick? Had Miss Miggs made him sick? Had he given the evidence to the police? Was he safe?

About half an hour into the day we began to realise that whatever had happened to Junior it wasn't anything good. I had my head down trying to solve a ridiculous maths problem when the door flew open and a large African lady burst into the room with Mr Potts and Mr Brown trying to restrain her.

'Where is he? What have you done with him?' she shouted.

'I don't know what you mean' replied Miss Miggs with an icy glare on her face as the snake began to wake up and slither around her chest.

'You were the last to see my boy. Your Principal has admitted it. Where is Junior? Where is my son?'

'I assure you I don't know what you're talking about. We brought Junior back to school with the other children and he left at the normal time.'

'No you didn't! You were with him in the caves and none of us saw you leave!' I shouted.

'Shut up Lily, Shut up!' screamed Miss Miggs.

'No, you're lying, you're an evil witch AND my name is Cookie Monster.'

'Bring me my son now,' demanded Junior's mother as she broke free of Mr Brown and Mr Potts diving at Miss Miggs and knocking her down to the floor. Everyone cheered this heroic act, but worryingly Miss Miggs was getting up and the snake was hissing. Junior's mom slapped Miss Miggs round the face and in return the snake struck and bit her arm. She didn't seem to care, she just slapped her again. Miss Miggs would have been helpless on the floor had it not been for her vicious snake and evil spells.

'Where is he? Tell me where my son is now!' Mr Brown tried to grab hold of her again, but she turned around and slapped him so hard that the big red nose flew off his face. Then Mr Potts tried to grab her and she slapped him the hardest. He went spinning around twice and then stumbling backwards and falling into a table. She grabbed the snake from the witch's neck and threw it at the window before grabbing hold of Miss Miggs' shocked body. Junior's mom was like superwoman. 'Did you leave him in the caves? Is he here? Tell me now. Where is my son?' she continued.

Suddenly a cold wind blew through the classroom, it was icy and terrifying. My attention was drawn away from the fighting to the doorway where several clouds of gas came creeping through the door. The gas was white almost like a cloud and the clouds were headed for Junior's mother. As they got closer and closer they twisted and swirled in the air. They were forming shapes, the shapes of human bodies. When they got right next to her they stopped moving and began to solidify into dark, sinister figures. Slowly the detail on them began to emerge. One was a tribal soldier, one a crazy nurse, one a businessman, one a pirate and one a wicked old drunk man. They all looked like they lived well over a hundred years ago. These sinister shapes grabbed Junior's mom and lifted her off the floor before they turned back into the white gas which began to float back out the door the way they had come. They were carrying Junior's mother as all the children screamed.

'This is not over. I will find my son.'

'It looks like they are taking you to see your precious son right now,' Mr

Brown sneered. He checked on Miss Miggs and Mr Potts before turning to the class in a rage. He grabbed someone's water bottle, poured some of it on his hands and wiped off all his clown make-up. Underneath it was just a normal man, quite handsome, but so angry and so sad. I could see it in his eyes.

'You want the real me? You want the truth? You want this school closed? You have no idea what would happen with this school closed. You are all at this school for a reason and you don't even know it. Junior wanted this school closed. We had to stop him. If any of you try to do what Junior did then you will be stopped as well.'

'Where is he?' I asked.

'He is safely tucked away for now. It is too dangerous to have him around. I know you were involved with what he was doing Cookie Monster.

When I have proof of it you will be going to the same place as Junior. If that brother of yours tries to stop us he will go there as well. This goes for everyone. Do not ask questions! Do not think about where you are! If you do there will be trouble. You are at the Halloween Horror School and you are never ever getting out. Do you understand?'

'Yes Mr Brown,' said most of the class. Not me though. I could tell we were finally getting to Mr Brown and we had to find Junior.

4 Days until Halloween
Rescue Dog

The days passed and there was still no sign of Junior or his mother, so desperate times called for desperate measures. Me and Josephine had concocted a plan to find them and we didn't waste much time in putting it into action.

At 3am on that chilly October night I sidled up to the creepy school with Scraps besides me. I felt confident that the place was now deserted of teachers, but I was worried that those hideous ghosts might still be around.

'Pssst Cookies. Over here!' came a voice from a large dead tree that twisted round in the centre with forked branches coming out at either side like bony arms and fingers.

'Josephine. Thank goodness you made it. I couldn't face it alone. How did you manage to get out?'

'My parents are deep sleepers, but I nearly didn't wake up myself. I've never been up at this time before. I don't like it, so quiet and empty.'

'I know. I had to listen out for Sam's snoring to be sure that he was asleep, but when I got outside it was dead silence. So creepy! Did you bring Junior's sports shirt?'

'Yes, he's always leaving things in school so I grabbed it on the way out.'

'Great! Now how are we going to get in?'

'The cooking room. It's windows are so old and rusty and there are vines growing through from outside. Mrs

Muddy is always complaining about how the windows don't shut.'

So we crept around the ghostly old building and sure enough with a little nudge the window opened up wide. I was looking forward to getting in as I was absolutely freezing and I really needed to warm up, but if anything once inside it was even more unbearably freezing. The window was quite small so I struggled to pull myself up and over and in. I landed on the floor with a bit of a bump and then I leaned back over the window to help Scraps get inside. Josephine followed us in and we made our way to the long winding corridors holding out Juniors T-shirt for Scraps to pick up the scent.

'Scraps find, find Junior, go,' I whispered and sure enough Scraps began making his way around the corridors with his nose firmly on the ground. We followed him quickly and I could not help having a huge smile on my face. 'What a good dog. You are amazing.'

Scraps slowed down and began to focus on a particular area. I watched as he lifted his head up and changed direction walking right into a closed door with a bump. Poor Scraps! He shook his head and continued sniffing round the door and at the crack at the bottom.

'He must have found him,' said Josephine opening the door to further darkness. When we grappled for the light switch we realised this was Mr Potts classroom as there were exercise bikes, medicine balls, skipping ropes and a giant treadmill in the classroom.

'He's not here.'

Scraps didn't seem so certain as he was sniffing around the room like crazy. He finally settled his attention around Mr Potts desk and we wasted no time in opening the drawers and having a proper good look. Yet there were no signs or clues that might lead us to Junior, each drawer was just stuffed to the brim with junk food. Mr Potts was a secret fatty! There were biscuits, cakes, donuts, sweets and chocolates. That was what Scraps had smelled! He grabbed a massive cake out of the drawer and wolfed it down.

'You naughty boy! You're supposed to be looking for Junior,' I said. We dragged Scraps outside. OK, so we helped ourselves to some of the biscuits first. I must admit as well as his acrobat skills Mr Potts had a pretty good taste in biscuits. We firmly closed the door to the classroom and got Scraps well away, then we tried one more time to get him to pick up the scent. Again we gave him the T-shirt and again he went skipping off with his nose and tail waggling all over the place. This time he was travelling much faster just stopping to try and dig at the wooden floor. He wanted to get lower. We ran around like this for what felt like forever and I started thinking we were going in circles until we ended up right at the back of the school and the big hall where Mr Brown gathered everyone to do his jokes and speeches. Scraps sniffed all over the floor and then stopped at a mat by the door. He was trying to dig under it so I lifted the mat. Hidden underneath we discovered a trap door. I grabbed hold of the lever on it and yanked as hard as I could until the cover flew off. We peered down, but it was so dark we couldn't see the bottom.

'Hello is anybody there there there?' my voice echoed as I called down the hole.

'Help help help,' came the echoed response.

Just as I was going to ask who it was I could feel again the icy cold wind that I'd experienced in class the other day. It blew through my hair and down into the tunnel. The door to the big hall slammed with a loud BANG and I froze in terror. From behind me I could hear the door opening again and I slowly turned my head to see if the ghosts were coming.

Cookies, Josephine you must get out of here now! The ghosts they are here,' came a familiar clackety clack voice. I turned around relieved that

Skelly had come to help us. 'We have to go, now!'

We all ran towards the door and I just about got through before it slammed shut again. I looked around relieved to see Skelly had made it and so had Josephine.

'Scraps!' I screamed as my little dog peered up at the door window in the door, blinking his big brown eyes and pressing his paws against the window. I tugged on the handle, but something had locked it. 'Scraps!'

'We have to go NOW,' spluttered Josephine as she pulled me away from the door and pointed at the white clouds of gas floating around us.

'I can't leave him,' I cried.

'We'll come back for him,' said Skelly. 'It's OK, they don't hurt you right away, but we won't be able to rescue anyone if we all get trapped.

We have to go before they turn human.'

We all sprinted as fast as we could as the gas clouds once again turned into the creepy figures from earlier. Through the corridors, up the main stairs and out.

'Keep running,' said Skelly. 'Don't stop until you get home. I will sort out this mess. We can try again soon to find them. I can't believe you came here so close to Halloween. The phantoms are out to play and they will get scarier. Run, home, now.

I ran so fast I thought my legs might fall off. Josephine had already run off for her house. I kept going until I was home. I sneaked back into the house and I crept upstairs before burying myself under my bed where I cried until morning.

1 day until Halloween
The Police

Sam noticed that Scraps wasn't there almost immediately. Of course he noticed what did I expect? I told him the whole story. I told him about Junior going missing on the school trip and I told him about the ghosts dragging his mum away. I told him about how we tried to use Scraps to find him and how the door had slammed shut on Scraps. So Sam drove us back to the school and again he spoke to Mr Potts and Miss Miggs. Of course, they were irritatingly nice to Sam again as if they were normal helpful teachers. Sam explained what I had told him and they looked at me

with pity as if I was a crazy girl
making up stories.

'Oh dear, what a tough time she's
been through,' said Miss Miggs, 'I'm
not surprised she is having these mad
thoughts. I can assure you Junior and
his mother are just fine. They went
back to Africa to visit Junior's
grandmother. He will be back at
school before Christmas. As for the
dog I'm afraid I have no idea, but I'm
afraid it is illegal to trespass on
school property and I should really
call the police if what you say is true.
I mean we don't want Lily getting in
trouble, but she can't break into the
school.'

'No don't call the police,' Sam said.

'I might have to, unless Lily admits
she was lying.'

'I'm not lying, look at her desk
there's a snakeskin. Look at the board.
496837.483 divided by 27.365. I

mean how is a kid supposed to answer that with no calculator? Everything I told you is true Sam, please believe me.'

'Well, then I'm afraid I have no choice. Lily has problems and we are running out of ways to help her. I must call the police,' said Miss Miggs.

'It's OK I think we are going to go to the police ourselves,' Sam said putting his arm around me and getting up to leave.

The next day we went down to the local police station and asked to see the number one man.

'We have many well trained police officers,' sighed the chubby man on the front desk.

'No, only the best will do,' demanded Sam. So the chubby man led us out into a big office past cops on phones and cops on computers and cops drinking coffee and eating donuts until we reached the back of this bustling room of chaos to a bright shiny door with a big star on it. Written on the star it said *Officer Mace policeman of the year for the tenth year.*

I immediately felt very reassured and confident that all my problems were to be solved by this heroic man. However, things are not always as they seem. When we went inside we were greeted by a guy wearing a Hawaiian shirt and baggy shorts instead of a police uniform. He told us to wait at the door as he carefully aimed some rubbish at a trash can like a professional basketball player. When he finally threw it he missed by a mile, before swearing and asking us to take a seat.

'Hello my name is Sam and this is Lily, we were told you were the best officer here.'

'Guilty,' said Officer Mace, 'I've made over 500 arrests this year alone and 412 of them did it.'

'What about the other 88,' I asked?

'They looked at me funny,' he said, 'now how can I help you?'

I went through the entire story from the first day at the Halloween Horror School right up to our meeting with Miss Miggs. Officer Mace listened patiently and scribbled down my story before reading it back to me to check it was accurate. It was really scary telling him all those things. Policeman are a bit like teachers, even the nice ones make you feel like you're in trouble when you haven't done anything.

'So you broke into the school?' said Officer Mace?

'Yes, but only to look for Junior.'

'Why didn't you come to us sooner?'

'Have you not been listening? I was scared. Those teachers are crazy and dangerous. I was scared of what they might do. We didn't have any evidence. Now we do, but it's with Junior and he's gone missing.' The phone in the office began to ring and Officer Mace excused himself to answer it. He made a lot of noises that could've meant anything. When he finally hung up he told us his colleague had said that Miss Miggs had just phoned to explain that they didn't want to press charges regarding breaking in and that Junior had returned to Africa for a short time. He said Miss Miggs was concerned about my mental health.

'My mental health? What does that mean?'

'Perhaps I could discuss that with your brother in private. We can arrange for you to speak to someone. A nice friendly person.'

'I'm not crazy. It's everyone else who is crazy,' I said. 'Are you not going to do anything about that school? Mr Brown is a nutter and the teachers are evil. I've told you what they've done and you sit there and say I'm crazy.'

'Calm down Lily, they want to help us,' Sam said.

'This idiot couldn't help a goldfish learn to swim. He's completely useless. I'm leaving this stupid place.'

Later that night a lady came round the house and asked me to tell her about the school again. Then she asked me to talk about my parents.

I'm not stupid though. They'll just use what I say against me, so I didn't say anything. When she left Sam asked me how he could help me. I just said that he should believe me.

'How can I believe you Lily? Listen to what you're saying,' Sam said as he walked off with tears in his eyes.

The next day I trudged to school wondering how I would ever get out of this terrible mess. It was a normal day and as boring, uncomfortable and difficult as ever, but just as the home time bell was about to go my life got much much worse.

We were called to an assembly and I fully expected to get custard pied and gunged by the teachers. Mr Brown appeared on stage and he was not in his clown suit and he was not making any jokes. His eyes were narrow and his lips were tight as he announced his warning to the school.

'As most of you now know this school has a large infestation of old ghosts and phantoms. Many of them that would normally be sleeping in the walls and underground decide to come out at Halloween. Halloween is tomorrow. All of these hidden ghosts are over two hundred years old and are very confused. They feel safe here and when something or someone threatens them they will take them away. If you do see an old ghost or phantom shut your eyes, do not look at them as you don't want them to feel scared or they will take you away with them. I'm telling you this a day early as they currently feel very threatened by two children who have recently seen them. One of these children even went to the police. It is my sad duty to tell you that they are coming for those children right now. So shut your eyes boys and girls, don't even peek, for the phantoms are on their way.'

Immediately children buried their faces in their arms as if someone had farted and they slammed their eyes shut. Out of panic I did the same and I looked over to make sure Josephine wasn't looking either.

I had my eyes closed so tight that my nose wrinkled up and all I could see were colourful spots through my eyelids. The hall was utterly silent and the atmosphere was thick with fear. The creak of the hall door shattered the quiet and so did the sound of someone actually doing a bottom burp.

Icy cold shivers of electricity pulsed through my body as I felt myself lifted up high into the air. The fear was so great that I opened my eyes to see myself flying through the air being carried by the white gas. I was looking down on all the other children who were cowering on the floor. Even Mr Brown and Mr Potts had their eyes shut. I turned my head the other way to see Josephine was also being carried across the great hall and out of the door. We were moving so fast now through the corridors up some stairs, through some classrooms, down other stairs where a trap door flew open. We were dragged down the trap door into pitch black before flying through some tunnels and into a big smelly room where a gate was slammed shut. Josephine was crying, but not me. I was angry.

The Ghost Dungeon

Sitting in a corner of that dark dingy cave I didn't care anymore. I'd been through so much that nothing could bother me anymore. A dark dungeon cave was just as good as a beautiful meadow with flowers to me. I was no longer scared of anything. My face was sad, my body was sad and my thoughts were sad until I had the most wonderful surprise. In the darkness I felt a wet nose press against my arm. I jumped before reaching out a hand to feel soft fur and a strong back.

'Scraps, Scraps is that you?'

'Woof,' came the reply.

'Scraps it is you. I've missed you so much,' I said as Scraps gave me a big hug and leaned against me. I patted his head and his back. 'It's OK Scraps. I'm OK. We're both going to be OK.'

After a while my eyes began to adjust to the darkness and I could see other familiar faces. Junior was facing a wall and bouncing a tennis ball against it. Further away was his mother comforting Josephine who was still crying a little bit.

'It's OK dear. I won't let them hurt you. You will be home with your parents very soon,' said Junior's mom as she held Josephine to her chest. 'Mr Brown has been down here and he said that the ghosts will let us go as soon as Halloween is over.'

'You can't trust him. He is worse than them. We have to get out of here, by ourselves,' came the voice of Junior who sounded more serious than I had ever heard him before.

'Be quiet Junior can't you see the poor girl is upset?'

'She needn't be upset,' he continued.
'I have a plan and tomorrow we are
getting out,'

'What's the plan?' I asked.

'I'll tell you in the morning. The old
ghosts and phantoms are listening at
night,' Junior said. Josephine stopped
crying and lay down by Junior's mum
for a sleep. As my eyesight adjusted
to the dark I could see more children
and a couple more parents were down
there with us. They were all sleeping
now and Scraps was also curling up for
a rest. The only person who wasn't
laying down was Junior and every time
I woke that night I saw him still
sitting in the same spot just bouncing
his tennis ball against the wall over
and over again.

Before I shut my eyes for bed I
made up a prayer to the universe.

The universe is big and bold,
Please let me live til I get old,

I'm not scared of ghosts or witches,
Those bad people have me in stitches,
My life has been so very tricky,
This situation's really sticky,
That Miss Miggs she smells like poo,
O universe what should I do?,
We want nice teachers, not Mr Brown,
Who wants a Principal who is a clown?
Mr Potts must stop his running,
We want a teacher bright and stunning,
As for Miss Miggs and her snake,
Please throw them in a stinky lake,
Please stop the bullies and their awful fights,
Help the lovely pure delights,
For at this school there are nice girls and boys,
And we deserve some marvellous toys,

I pray to you to keep us well,
Old Mr Brown will rot in hell,
The world is such a lovely place,
But it's hidden by this school
disgrace,
All I wants is a little help and
bravery,
To stop these teachers keeping kids
in slavery,
It's up to me to save the day,
So with your help I won't delay,
I can stop this, I know I can,
So universe give me a plan,
While you're at it help everyone,
Who is suffering and needs some
fun,
Help the animals do their thing,
Help the birds to fly and sing,
I know you'll help me sort this out,
That's what the universe is all
about.

God bless everyone.

Halloween

I have always loved Halloween, it's so much fun. I remember one Halloween where I made jack o lanterns with my parents and then we bobbed for apples. My dad was really good at apple bobbing. He would grab it almost immediately then pull his face out of the water and shake his head like a wet dog. Then I would get dressed up in a scary costume. It was funny how I remembered some of my old costumes being that of a witch and a clown. I would never be dressing like that again.

It was difficult to tell when morning finally arrived as no light could enter the dark underground tunnels or the cage in which I currently found myself. Around me I could see the shadows of people waking up and I wondered how they had been filling in their time stuck in the dungeon all day everyday. I wished I had a tennis ball to bounce like Junior as I was already getting fidgety and bored. However, when I looked over at Junior he wasn't bouncing his ball the way he had been ever since I had been stuck in this terrible prison. When I looked over to him he was kneeling down holding onto his stomach and he seemed to be chanting or praying or something.

His mother had gone over to see what was wrong with him and he said that he felt his belly was going to explode.

'I'm not surprised with this yucky food they give us,' his mum said holding up a dry piece of bread and the leg of some unknown creature. It definitely wasn't chicken. 'You need some of my home cooking inside you.'

'Don't talk about food, it hurts too much,' Junior moaned as he rolled over to his side and let out the most hideous groan of agony. He sounded like a wounded warthog as he kept rolling around like a pig in poo. These moans and groans got worse and worse as he went from these backwards and forward rolls to kneeling down with his head on the floor. One time he stood up and breathed deeply a few times, but when he breathed in really deep he quickly grabbed his stomach again and collapsed to the floor. 'Its agony,' he gasped 'it's so painful.'

'He needs a doctor,' Jospehine said.

'He's going to explode and his insides are going to splatter all over us,' said another kid in the jail.

'He needs a doctor,' said Junior's mum.

'Woof,' said Scraps. I agreed with them all.

'We need to get him to a doctor. If we all shout loud enough somebody will hear us,' said Junior's mum. So after she gave the count of three we all cried out as hard as we could. 'Heeeeellllllllpp!!!' we screamed and then it went quiet again, but for Junior's moans and groans. 'Heeelllp,' we screamed again, 'he's dying, he's going to explode!'

For such a long time there was no answer and our cries gained no response, but for a creepy echo through the tunnels and a panic in Junior that made him groan and moan even more. Slowly people started to give up until only Josephine and Junior's mum continued. Eventually our calls were answered, but by the two people I least wanted to see.

I couldn't see them coming, but I could hear them. That creepy laugh began as an echo before getting clearer and clearer and louder and louder. 'Hooo hoo haa ha ho hee haa,' it went.

I walked up to the rusty iron bars of the cage and peered into the darkness. There was nothing there, yet I was sure that laugh was getting closer. I blinked to try and adjust my eyes to the far away darkness, but when I opened them I didn't need to look that far. Mr Brown with his clown face was just inches in front of me. His massive grin revealed dazzling white teeth as saliva ran down from the corners of his mouth. His eyes were piercing and hypnotic. I could not stand to look at them so I backed away quickly and tripped over Junior who was still kneeling in pain. As I fell over the top of him he groaned even louder. It sounded like a polar bear was being microwaved.

'What is going on? Why all the screaming? You are going to wake the ghosts up too early. Heaven knows there will be enough of them today anyway,' said Miss Miggs.

'It is my boy. His stomach, he is in pain. He needs a doctor,' said Junior's mum.

'Do you think we care?' sneered Miss Miggs. We don't care if he has sharks in his tummy eating him from the inside out.'

'You will care when you have hundreds of policeman and doctors in this place. Eventually people will look for us. That story about us going back to Africa won't last forever. What about the people looking for Josephine and Cookies and all these people? You can't keep us here much longer.'

'We are only keeping you here until after Halloween. The old ghosts have ordered it and you must stay.'

'Hang on a second Miss Miggs,' said Mr Brown. 'This hilarious lady is correct. If Junior is really sick then he must see a doctor. He must see a doctor immediately. Fortunately at Clown College I took several courses in medicine. Yes, I will operate on Junior immediately. Let's get him to my office. Perhaps I can also do some dentistry on him. After all that is my favourite.'

'You will not touch my son you wicked man.'

'Open the door Miss Miggs,' ordered Mr Brown as Junior continued to cry out in pain. Miss Miggs pulled out a heavy set of keys that I could hear rattling away. She put a large key into the lock before realising it was the wrong one and began searching for the correct one. Eventually there came the click and the squeak as the rusty old door swung open and the vile teachers entered. In the hazy darkness I saw the two wretched villains grab Junior under the arms and drag him to his feet.

'Now!' shouted Junior like a Gladiator king uttering a command and the room sprang into violent chaos. Scraps dived for Mr Brown and sunk his teeth deep into his leg.

'A ha aha ohooo hoo ho hee,' came the sound from old clown Brown. Junior's mum grabbed Miss Miggs, picked her up and threw her against the wall like a rag doll whilst all of the kids and parents barged their way out of the cell trampling old Miggs and Brown.

'Where are the keys? We have to lock them in,' said Junior. We all looked around, but we couldn't see them anywhere.

'Forget it, they are starting to get up. Just run everybody. Run as fast as you can!' Josephine said. So we ran like crazy. We ran through the tunnels desperately searching for a ladder or some stairs to take us up and out. It seemed to take forever and the mad chuckling was echoing again. The crazy teachers were definitely after us.

Finally a ray of hope. A rope up to another trap door. One at a time we climbed up and out. Junior went first followed by his mum and then the other parents and kids.

'I'm going to get help. I'm going to the police,' said Junior.

Some parents dropped a big bucket down that was tied to a rope and we put Scraps in the bucket and they pulled him up.

The last boy started pulling his way up the rope, but he was really finding it hard. Just as he neared the top he began sliding down again and he had to start his slow climb once more.

'Hurry up, we don't have much time,' I pleaded as I heard the clown laugh really loudly in my ears. 'We don't have time, start climbing Josephine.' It was just me and her left at the bottom. She got two pulls up when Miss Miggs went flying through the air grabbed her off the rope, did a somersault and landed on her feet with her arms holding Josephine in a headlock. Then I felt a big white smelly hand cover my mouth and face as I was dragged away from the rope by the clown. The boy was pulled up by the long arm of his father, but Josephine and I weren't going anywhere.

Mr Brown's Secret

We were dragged up and down winding corridors; we turned left and right until I totally lost where I was. Eventually we were taken up some concrete stairs through Mr Brown's evil closet and into his office, where we were made to sit on chairs with thumbtacks on them. Mr Brown wasted no time in making two custard pies and slamming them into our faces before taking his own seat at his desk. He took some deep nasal breaths before beginning to talk.

'I'm afraid you two will not be allowed out of this school for at least 48 hours. Believe me I wish it wasn't true as I'm sick of the sight of both of you. Josephine you used to be so well behaved. You were a quiet little girl who was bullied without complaint. You failed miserably at your work and you caused no problems. What's happened to you?'

'I had enough. I remembered my school in Colombia and how much happier I was there.'

'Oh yes the school in Colombia. Well you know as well as I do that you can never return there. And Lily, Cookie Monster, since starting this school you've caused nothing but trouble. I thought you would start to toe the line, I thought you were learning, but not only have you disobeyed my rules time and time again, you have woken far too many old ghosts and now I am sure I will have the police to deal with.'

'That's right and they will lock you up. See how you like being in a cage,' I said.

'Hoo heee haha ha,' laughed Mr Brown. 'I don't think you know who you're dealing with. Do you think I don't know how to deal with the police? I've had them visit many times before and there is never anything they can do about this school.'

'Well we have evidence and you have broken sooooo many laws. So this time it will be different I guarantee.'

'Hahoheehahoo, you still don't know do you? You have no idea what's going on here, either of you.'

'What do you mean? What is going on here?' I asked.

'Do you think that was the real police you went to see the other day?' Mr Brown asked with his most menacing grin ever.

'Of course, what else would they be?'

'The ghost police.'

'The ghost police? You're crazy. You're completely mad,' I laughed.

'You don't believe me, read this.' Mr Brown pulled out a newspaper clipping and shoved it under my pie encrusted nose.

SUPERCOP KILLED SAVING CAT
Last night local police officer Gregory Mace died rescuing a little boy's cat from a large oak tree. Officer Mace had just arrested twenty-seven criminals who were fighting in town and had earlier that day found evidence to convict Europe's biggest criminal known as Dastardly Dave. Other police officers described Mace as a fun and brave man. Mace had climbed twenty metres up the massive tree before grabbing the cat when the branch snapped and he fell to the ground. He miraculously managed to cradle and protect the cat in his arms. The cat survived, but Officer Mace did not. They owner of the cat says he is so grateful that

Officer Mace saved his friend and will remember him always.

'I still don't believe he's a ghost, but if he is we'll just go tell a real policeman,' I said.

'I'm afraid that's impossible,' Mr Brown said.

'Why?'

'Haven't you guessed it yet? Because you, both of you, everyone you've met at this school. Everyone you know. You're all ghosts hahooheehoha.'

'But that's impossible. We've seen the real ghosts and we're nothing like them.'

'Those ghosts are different. They have been ghosts for centuries and have special powers.'

'So I suppose you're a ghost too.'

'Well yes. I'm not a trained teacher. I was a clown and I was shot out of a canon about forty years ago. It all went wrong. I was shot right into a wall and I came here. I started as a dinner lady. I mean dinner man, but I got so good at being evil they made me the Principal.'

'Who made you the Principal?'

'The old ghosts, the ones that turn to gas, the phantoms. The ones you've seen. All the teachers here are ghosts. Mr Potts died trying to run twenty five marathons in one day. He got to seventeen and then collapsed. The only teacher who is not a ghost is Miss Miggs. She's a witch.'

'What about Skelly?'

'Skelly? Clearly he's a ghost. He died in 1888 in a fire. Aren't you more interested in the other children? Burgers died from eating too much, Ladders died from falling off a ladder. They are all ghosts. Your little friend Junior died of malnutrition in Africa and his mother was so broken-

hearted that she died soon after.
This is a school for ghost children.'

'What about us, what happened to
us?' asked Josephine.

'You Josephine, well you are lucky.
Your whole family died together, so
you are all ghosts. You were on holiday
in Asia when there was a Tsunami that
drowned you.'

'And me?' I asked.

'Your family were in a car crash, but
your parents were wearing seatbelts,
it was you and your brother who died.'

'That's not true. It was me and my
brother who survived the crash.
You're lying.'

'Think about it Cookies. Think about
the strange things that live in your
garden. They couldn't possibly survive
here. They are ghost plants and
animals. Look at the hippos in the
school. Hippos don't live in this
country. They are also ghosts.'

'I suppose that would make sense, but I still know you're lying,' I said.

'Of course it makes sense, I hope now you understand why you must stay here until after Halloween. You have angered the older ghosts and you must miss the fun of Halloween as punishment. They put you in that dungeon so they could tell you off today and they still want to do that.'

'I suppose that's fair,' said Josephine as we sat there utterly confused.

Maybe Mr Brown was telling us the truth. How else could I explain all the strange things that had been going on? I never even thought about why my house was so unusual. My house didn't make any sense. How can it shoot into the air? What were hippos doing in the school, not to mention a skeleton librarian? Suddenly it all made sense, everything was clear. I was dead. I was a ghost and my parents were still alive.

'Do you know anything about my dog? Do you know anything about Scraps?' I asked.

'Yes, he's not really your dog. He belonged to a homeless man in Brazil, but he was run over. I don't know how he ended up in your house. You must have picked him up at the ghost dog shelter. Now I have lots to do, this is the busiest day of the year for me. It's Halloween and I have lots of humans to scare tonight. I must be going. I will lock you two in here. The phantoms will be here to tell you off fairly soon. I'll let you out again in a couple of days and from then on, you will start to behave. Everyone always does.'

Mr Brown got up and headed towards the door. Josephine and I just sat there dumbfounded and in shock as the door closed behind us and we were locked in.

'Maybe it's true. I do remember a big wave and being underwater,' said Josephine, 'it was awful.

Trapped

The noisy nastiness of a ringing fire alarm made me hold onto my ears. The shocking noise woke me up from the most terrible thoughts, the thought that my whole life was a lie and that I was a ghastly ghost. I got up and looked out of the window to see Junior leading a mob of children out of the school. He turned back and although I couldn't hear him I think I could lip read what he was saying to the other children.

'Run, be free. Get away from the Halloween Horror School,' or something like that. He was leading an exodus and I wanted to be a part of it. I started banging on the windows and trying to get their attention, but there must have been three layers of glass and outside the glass were metal bars. There was no way anyone would hear me and who looks back when they're running out of a horror school? Nobody. We were stuck.

I ran to the door and started banging on it. I banged my fists on the door over and over again calling for help, but no-one came. Josephine was still just sitting in her chair frozen in disbelief.

'I'm a ghost. My family are ghosts. Everyone at my school is a ghost. Everyone I know is a ghost. Oh my goodness,' she said.

'Josephine, get up. We have to get out of here. It's Halloween and it won't be long until it gets dark. There will be so many old ghost phantoms here,' I said.

'We are ghosts. What difference does it make? Maybe we need to be told off.'

'Maybe we're not ghosts. Maybe Mr Brown was lying.'

'It must be true. It all makes sense. We must be ghosts.'

'Whatever. We still need to get out of here. Do you really want to stay here and be told off by those old ghosts? Do you want to be stuck with them all night on Halloween?'

'I suppose not, no, that sounds dreadful.'

'Then help me figure out how to get out of here.' We both went quiet and into deep thought. I was wracking my brain for an answer. Maybe there was another secret passageway or a trap door. I tried to open the door leading to Mr Brown's closet that we came through, but that was locked too. The windows were thick and the floor was strong. 'We could throw a chair at the window,' I suggested.

'Even if it breaks we won't get past the iron bars,' Josephine said.

'Then we'll have to break down this door somehow.'

'If we really are ghosts then why would we need to break the door down? Can't ghosts walk through walls and sink or rise through ceilings? If we are ghosts then we can just walk straight through that wall,' Josephine said moving towards the wall to do exactly what she said. She moved nervously and awkwardly like a baby deer walking away from its mummy. 'Bang!' she cracked her head right on the wall and walked away holding her nose. 'Ow ow ow!' she cried.

'Maybe you have to do it with a bit more belief. You know, really believe you're going to go through the wall,' I said walking right to the other side of the room for a good long run up. 'I am a ghost. I can run through doors. I am a ghost. I can run through walls,' I told myself as I began sprinting at the door. Boom! 'Ow ow ow!' I cried rolling around on the floor. 'My head, my beautiful head. I've broken it. We're not ghosts Mr Brown was lying.'

'No, but they are,' gasped Josephine pointing to the white gas floating through the wall. I sprang to my feet and started kicking on the wooden door as hard as I could. It wasn't budging. I took a run up as the gases began forming into human figures and jumped into the air giving the door my hardest flying kick ever. I felt the bottom of my foot connect with the door and this time it moved. It swung violently open and I heard another massive bang as I crashed to the floor. Mr Brown was on his way back in. My big kick had sent the door smashing into his nose, his normal nose. He'd come back to collect the red nose he'd left in his drawer. Now he had a red nose for real.

'That was amazing Cookie Monster. Now let's get out of here,' Josephine said as I looked up to see the ugly old nurse ghost try to grab my arms. I rolled out of the way as Josephine barged the door open hitting Mr Brown who was now lying on the floor. We squeezed our way past him as the ghosts began to chase us.

The Chase

'I'll get you for this,' cried Mr Brown
as he tried to stop us getting past his
legs by tripping us up. We leapt over
him and ran, through the waiting room
and out into the big corridor as the
icy cold ghost breath scraped across
our backs. Miss Miggs was waiting at
the end of the corridor and she called
for us to stop. We darted left to
avoid running right into her and she
gave chase as well.

'Stop now or I will use my magic,'
Miss Miggs called, but she'd already
begun. Poisoned frogs began falling
from the ceiling making us duck and
dart our way forward in an attempt to
avoid
them.

A green and yellow one landed on my shoulder with a plop, but I pushed him off before he had a chance to get me. Next there were spikes popping up from the floor. They were razor sharp and would have gone straight through our feet had we stepped on one, but luckily we were both really good at dodging them. 'You asked for it! Time for the quicksand.' Suddenly the floor of the corridor turned from stone into sloppy, thick, heavy quicksand. My front foot landed in it and began to sink and with my other leg I went down to one knee. I desperately tried to pull my legs out, but they wouldn't budge.

'Don't put your hands in it,' warned Josephine. 'Your arms will get stuck. I read 'Escaping Quicksand' by Sandy Stickfeet in the library a couple of weeks ago. We need something to pull ourselves out with.'

Behind us the ghosts and Mr Brown were sinking too, so was Miss Miggs and Mr Potts appeared from his classroom trying to help her, but then he got stuck very rapidly.

'I can get out of this no problems,' bragged Mr Potts, 'I'm a fitness master.' The ghost phantoms were beginning to turn into gas again. They would be able to fly right over us and get us. Probably for the best as we were sure to sink otherwise. As I fought and struggled I sank faster and faster. I looked back again and Miss Miggs was beginning to rise out of the quicksand. She reached up into the air and her whole body seemed to follow; she began to levitate and then fly.

'Enough games I'm going to straighten you out once and for all,' said Miss Miggs as her big ugly pointy toed feet came crashing down on my shoulders. She bounced off me and onto Josephine who she hammered deeper into the sand. Then she bounced back onto me again and I was pushed in right up to my chest. I couldn't help putting my arms in for support as Miss Miggs clattered into me again and again. She thumped Josephine just as hard. A couple more hard landings and we would both be totally submerged in the sand. I began to say my prayers.

'Get off them you wicked witch.' The library door had flung open by our right and Skelly was fiddling with his hand. He yanked his left hand right off his arm bone and squashed it into a fist before throwing it at Miss Miggs. It hit her right on the chest and she flew backwards.

'Cookies, Josephine. Climb over me and into the library. I opened a window that leads into the playground.

Go as quick as you can,' Skelly said before turning round and then falling flat on his back onto the quicksand. I mustered all my strength to pull one arm out of the sand and reached forward with all my might. I put my fingers in Skelly's eye sockets and pulled. I slowly struggled the other arm out of the sand and grabbed onto his shoulder and pulled. I was able to use his ribcage like a ladder pulling myself closer and closer to the library. As I crawled and pulled I manage to get the entire top half of my body out and lunged for his bony leg. With two more pulls my leg was free. I crawled into the library and grabbed a skipping rope from the lunchtime bag and threw it for Josephine. She managed to grab hold of it and I slowly pulled her in. The ghosts by now had floated into the library and were beginning to move down from the ceiling towards ground level ready to turn human again. The teachers were stuck in the sand.

'Cancel that spell you silly woman. I will fire you from the Horror school if you don't make this floor back into concrete,' cried Mr Brown.

'I'm sinking, i'm sinking,' cried Mr Potts and he really was. He'd tried so hard to run, jump and swim his way out that all I could see that was left of him was his mouth, nose and the top of his head sticking out of the quicksand. Miss Miggs immediately cancelled the spell and the quicksand turned back to stone. The only problem was so did Mr Potts. The ground was totally flat stone, but for a headshaped bump in the middle of the corridor. It was a 'Mr Potts' bump. A few feet further back I could see Mr Brown from the waist up, but his legs and bottom had been trapped in the stone floor as well.

'Get me out of here Miss Miggs. This is your final warning.'

We didn't have time to wait around as the ghosts were turning human again. We raced to the window to try to escape. As I peered out at the top of a tree I realised we were not on the ground floor. We were high up and there was a slanted roof outside the window that sloped down to a big drop to the floor. It looked like a terrifyingly long way down to the grass below.

'What are we going to do?' I asked.

'Remember we're ghosts it won't hurt us,' said Josephine climbing up onto the window ledge.

'Are you crazy? That drop will kill us,' I said.

'Ghosts can't be killed by falling, but they might be killed by those other ghosts. I'm jumping,' said Josephine as she climbed out of the window and lay down on the sloping roof.

'Wait, I'm coming too,' I said as I turned back to see the pirate on his way towards me with a sword. To make matters worse the other ghosts were almost fully human again.

We lay on the roof and counted down – 3-2-1 then we rolled. We started off slowly, but I guess gravity must have taken over because soon I was spinning round and round so fast that I couldn't stop myself. Suddenly the roof was gone and I was free-falling. I braced myself for the landing, but wasn't brave enough to open my eyes. When the impact came it wasn't an agonising thud to the ground, but a soft springy feeling like falling on a bouncy castle. I went up again before landing with a softer bounce off and onto the floor ending with just a little bump. I'd fallen on one of the hippos and he'd collapse under my weight. Miss Miggs must have sent a spell to get them there to stop our escape. The hippo looked mad when he got to his feet and he charged at me, so I moved out of the way as quick as a flash. I knew he wouldn't stop until he'd run me over so I jumped on top of his back again and held on for dear life. Josephine had her own problems with the hippo that she had landed on.

'Get on him and hold tight,' I shouted. It's the only way he won't trample you. So Josephine climbed on her hippo too and they started running around trying to shake us off. After so much running, climbing out of quicksand and not having eaten in so long it was hard work not to fall off that hippos back I can tell you.

Eventually, the animals seemed to calm down and give up on trying to shake us off. They just began walking slowly towards their lake for a drink, but I was terrified to get off in case they got angry again. I also thought with loads of ghosts, a clown and a witch chasing me that being on the back of a hippo was probably the safest place to be.

We walked around the lake for a bit which gave us a moment's silence and a break from the fear. It seemed terribly peaceful until the hippos took a plodding step into the dirty brown lake followed by another one. They wanted a swim. We slid off the hippos and onto the muddy bank as they went deeper and deeper into the water until all we could see were their little ears poking above the surface. Josephine and I just collapsed on the bank and I didn't even care that I was laying face first in squelchy pooey mud. I just wanted to sleep and for a brief second that is what I did.

'Hoo hee ha hah ho!' came the mad laugh of Mr Brown. I opened my one eye that hadn't sunk in the mud and saw the bright colours of Mr Browns costume and his crazy white smile. I pulled my head out of the filth and opened the other eye to see Miss Miggs standing just behind him. 'We've got you now; there is no escape. What a silly day to be naughty on hoo hee ha, Halloween at the Halloween Horror School. If I were you I would have behaved very well today, but now it's too late. It's now dark and all the old ghosts have woken up.'

Out of the darkness behind Mr Brown and Miss Miggs hundreds, maybe thousands of white gas clouds were becoming more bright and visible. They settled down and arranged into more solid shapes before making different forms of life. Most were human, but others were not. There were crocodiles, gorillas, komodo dragons and emu's, in fact all the really violent nasty animals were there. As colours and details began to form on the human ghosts it was clear that none of them were particularly pleasant either. There were prisoners, drunks, bullies, gangsters, pirates and lawyers. They were all horrible to look at. I tapped Josephine on the shoulder and she too began to wake up.

'They've got us now Josephine. Thanks for being my friend. It's all over.' I said as I closed my eyes and waited for whatever terrible thing they would do.

War of the Ghosts

Halloween isn't always as cold as you might think. Sometimes it's quite warm and the only thing to remind you its autumn is the wind blowing leaves off the trees and the terrible darkness that comes far too early and stays far too late. Covered in mud and quicksand, however, I was terribly cold that particular Halloween night.

'Let's make them walk the plank,' a pirate with an eye patch and a cackling parrot said.

'No, just get them into my horse and carriage,' said a man with a black medical bag, a sharp knife and a black cape. I think he might have been Jack the Ripper.

'Og ug og ug,' bellowed a bully from caveman times as he waved his club in the air and beat his chest.

'Dies sind schlechte kinder,' demanded Adolf Hitler as spit flew out of his angry mouth and he held his hand in the air.

'They snitched on us to the police, now we gotta beat them up,' said Al Capone smoking a cigar and punching his right fist into his left hand.

'You can do all those things,' said Mr Brown turning to the group of thugs behind him, 'but this is a school so just get into a nice line behind me and my custard pies, hoo ha hee hoo.'

'Oh no!' said Josephine.

Suddenly a bright light appeared in the sky and I looked up to see flowers falling - large petal shaped objects falling down to the ground. Everyone looked up to see what the shapes were that were about to land around us. My face went from an utterly miserable sadness to the brightest smile ever when I saw that the shapes were soldiers, brave soldiers from World War 2 parachuting in to rescue us. You see it's not just the bad ghosts that come out at Halloween. Not many people know that. All the wonderful amazing people can come out as well and these ones had come to save us.

As the first man landed he unhooked his parachute and ran straight into the crowd of nasty ghosts and started hitting them with his rifle. Others landed and joined in the fight against badness. Soon there was fighting everywhere and I quickly found myself wishing they would all just stop. Even after everything this huge battle was by far the scariest thing I'd been around and I didn't like it one little bit. I desperately wanted it to end, but every time I dared to open my eyes there were weapons being thrown around, bombs going off and people hurting each other. I pleaded for it to stop as I lay there quiet and helpless. I hoped they would leave me alone if they thought I was already hurt so I just lay there frozen, not wanting to move a muscle.

After what felt like a lifetime I felt a hand on my shoulder, it was a young handsome soldier and he wasn't alone. He had a rather large backpack and poking out of the top of it was a familiarly cheeky face.

'These are the kids we are here to rescue,' Junior said as he poked his head high out of the soldier's bag like a tortoise. 'Over there, that is Miss Miggs kicking your colonel and that is Mr Brown, the man hopping around in the explosions and laughing to himself,'

Junior had done a good job of getting help, but I wish things didn't have to be so violent.

'Affirmative, send in the reinforcements,' said the handsome soldier to his radio. Within moments there were trucks full of new people arriving, these people weren't in army uniforms. They looked like a wide range of normal people and none of them looked like they wanted to fight. As the new people arrived so did new animals. A whole host of brave, strong and wise looking animals had come to stop this awful ghost war.

'Ghosts! Stop fighting! An eye for an eye will make the whole world blind,' said a man dressed in nothing but white sheets. His name was Ghandi and as he spoke the noise of the war died down as more and more ghosts began to listen to him. 'What you hate about your enemy is what you really hate about yourselves. If you don't like something simply stop it yourself. Be the change you want to see in the world. You don't like fighting so don't fight. You don't like liars so don't lie. Be the person you want others to be.' As Ghandi reached the end of his speech there were only a few people left fighting. Josephine and I finally felt brave enough to get out of the mud and stand up as Ghandi said 'Nobody can hurt us without our permission.'

From behind Ghandi a very friendly, but serious man stepped out from behind him and began to speak. 'I have a dream that man and ghost will be treated as equals,' this man's name was Dr Martin Luther King and his voice stopped the last few cavemen and pirates who were still trying to fight the soldiers and each other. 'This is not going to happen if we are fighting amongst ourselves. We are one, we must stand as one. We must care for all our fellow ghosts no matter who they are! Or where they come from! Then, just maybe we can live free, in peace.'

Then another man came forward. His hair was absolutely crazy like he'd just got out of bed. But he had these big bright intelligent eyes and I couldn't wait to hear what he'd say.

'My name is Albert Einstein and I must say I believe Dr King is correct. We are the same as humans. We are the same as each other. We are all part of the same universe and to help and love your fellow ghost is to love and help yourself. To fight others is to fight your self and that is madness.'

The fighting totally stopped as lions, leopards, elephants and rhinos got in between the two sets of ghosts and everything became calm. Some of the ghosts even started hugging each other. Jack the Ripper began playing fetch with a wolf, Al Capone was asking the soldiers how he could help them and I'm sure I even saw Adolph Hitler cuddling a tree.

For the first time in ages I felt warmth in my heart and I began to smile

The Ghost Princess

Now that everyone was calm and peaceful it was time for the final visitor at the Halloween Horror School. A big shiny car slowly pulled up to the back of the school field, that had just become a battleground and several people lined up to open the door. An elegant leg emerged from the car before a tall slim woman with short blonde hair stepped out wearing a crown full of precious jewels. I thought it looked incredibly dangerous to wear a crown with so many pirates and thieves around, but she didn't look in the slightest bit worried. It wasn't until I saw her beautiful blue eyes sparkle that I realised I was looking at Princess Diana.

'Why must you make us come out every Halloween to stop you being naughty?' asked Princess Diana to the crowd of listening ghosts. 'This year you've really gone too far. Hiding in a school, being horrible to children, there is no excuse for it. I know you all had difficult lives, but you shouldn't take it out on others.'

'We can't help it. Its fun being horrible,' said a man with his legs shackled together. He was wearing black and white stripey prison clothes.

'Don't forget funny, it's funny too,' said a man with a briefcase.

'You've had so many chances to be good and do good things, but you keep choosing to be wicked. This year you are not going to get away with it,' explained Princess Diana.

'But its Halloween,' said a man in a suit with loads of money coming out of his many pockets.'

'I understand that it's Halloween. I myself am going to make lots of people jump later on. Its jolly good fun, but I won't have you being mean and confusing children. They weren't fun scared they were really scared and we can't have that.' As the kind Princess spoke everyone turned to look at me and Josephine, both of us shivering and filthy and there was a loud cry of 'sorry!'

'I'm glad you have said sorry, but this time it is not enough. For the next year each of you will pair up with a friend who is completely different to you and you will learn from each other. Criminals you will live with soldiers. You will learn discipline and respect. Animals you will live together in peace; you will like each other for your differences. Pirates you will live with tribes people, people who don't care about money and treasure. You will learn that the only treasure worth caring about is the gold in the heart of yourselves and others. Businessmen and lawyers you will live with gardeners and craftsmen and you will learn of beauty and nature.'

'What about them, they made children come here, what will happen to Miss Miggs and Mr Brown?' asked Junior who had climbed out of the soldier's bag and sidled up to stand by the Princess. Miss Miggs and Mr Brown had been handcuffed by Officer Mace and were looking very sad.

'I think we will need some special people to fix their wicked ways, don't you?' said Diana putting her hand on Juniors' shoulder. 'Miss Miggs you are not a ghost, you are a witch. You have incredible powers that could be used for good. Instead you use them for bad. You are going to live with Mother Teresa and she will teach you to be kind.'

'Oh no, please. I don't want to be kind. Please don't make me go with her!' said Miss Miggs as Mother Teresa came running up through the crowds of people and took Miss Miggs by the hand. She began speaking in a soft voice and pulled out a medical bag. She seemed to think Miss Miggs was sick or injured because of all the warts, so she started wrapping her in bandages. She was really quick and she went round and round Miss Miggs until she'd wrapped her from head to toe and all you could see was one mummified witch. 'I'll get you for this! Especially you naughty children. This isn't the end of me,' mumbled Miss Miggs through the bandages.

'As for you Mr Brown, you need to learn of some better comedy. You will be spending the year with Charlie Chaplin,' said Diana as a funny little man with a moustache and a bowler hat began waddling over to Mr Brown swinging a long stick made of bamboo. He introduced himself by taking off his hat then took Mr Brown's clown nose off and dropped it on the floor. When Mr Brown bent down to pick it up Charlie Chaplin kicked him up the bum. Then he did it again. It was brilliant and all the ghosts laughed.

'Ouch, I don't like it when people do jokes on me,' cried Mr Brown. When Mr Brown tried to walk away Charlie Chaplin tripped him up with his walking stick and then picked him up and gave him a big kiss on the cheek.

'No anyone but him. I beg you,' spluttered Mr Brown.

<u>Rewards</u>

'Now as we go away to our separate places with our new friends,' said Princess Diana, 'let me remind all of you ghosts that apart from a few funny jokes on Halloween you are not to bother humans this year. As it is Halloween right now I want to start celebrating and i'm sure you all have some jokes to be playing so we can all go just as soon as we have some well deserved medals given to these brave children who uncovered this awful school.'

A tall man with a beard and a big top hat came over to Josephine, Junior and I carrying the biggest, shiniest medals. They were much shinier than the Olympic ones. He came up to each one of us individually and placed the medals over our heads and dropped them so that they sat proudly across our chests.

'Thank you Cookie Monster. Thank you Josephine. Thank you Junior. You have proved something was true when I was alive, just as its true today. You have proved that there is nothing to fear, but fear itself and the world is always grateful to know that.'

Behind Mr Lincoln was Princess Diana who wanted to shake our hands and give us a warm hug. When she got to Junior she bent down and gave him a kiss on the cheek.

'Oh yuck,' protested Junior, but afterwards he couldn't stop smiling.

Out of the crowds came Josephine's parents, Juniors' mum and for me came Sam and Scraps. They all gave us a big cuddle and it felt so warm after everything that had happened. We drove home and Sam cooked me the yummiest dinner ever. It was roast beef with potatoes, vegetables and gravy. After I'd had that we made cookies and I must have had about a thousand of them. Mmmmm Cookies.

I had a nice hot bath and got into my pyjamas ready for bed. Burning in the corner of my room was a grinning pumpkin that Sam had carved. I quickly blew it out as i'd had quite enough of Halloween. As the light in my room faded, a huge light shone in my room from outside and it was followed by a deafening rumble. I ran to my window to see planes flying in the sky and smoke coming from the distance. They had blown up the school and I would never have to go there again.

Sam and Scraps came to tuck me in and although the ghost police had told my brother all that had happened I wanted to give my version of events, so I told him everything. He listened patiently and patted my head to comfort me. I finished the story by asking the question that I'd been thinking about since we were stuck in Mr Brown's office.

'Are we really ghosts?'

'No of course not,' said Sam. 'We are living humans. We've just had a lot of bad luck.'

'But what about everything Mr Brown said? It doesn't make any sense.'

'I'll explain everything I promise. Mr Brown was just trying to scare you. Right now you need to sleep.'

'OK,' I said blinking my eyes slower and slower. As Sam turned off my bed side light and stood up I managed to open my eyes one last time before drifting off to sleep. Maybe I was dreaming, I still don't know, but I'm

sure I saw Sam and Scraps
disintegrate into two white clouds of
gas.

I hope I was dreaming.

8063029R00129

Printed in Great Britain
by Amazon.co.uk, Ltd.,
Marston Gate.